Possessed by Magic

Thorne Sisters Chronicles
Book One

RENEE JOINER

Oshun
Publications

Contents

Book Design by MMB
Published by Oshun Publications
www.oshunpublications.com

Did you know you can take every story with you?

I know it's tough these days to simply find the time to relax and curl up with a good book. This is why I'm delighted to share that I have books available in audio book format.

Best of all, you can get the audio book version of any book by me for free as part of a 30-day Audible trial.

Members get free audio books every month and exclusive discounts. It's an excellent way to explore and determine if audio book learning works for you.

If you're not satisfied, you can cancel anytime within the trial period. You won't be charged, and you can even keep your audio book.

To choose a free audio book, click on your favorite title's cover to be taken to Audible's website for details.

Remember, there's no obligation to buy.

reneejoinerauthor.com/audiobooks

JOIN MY
NEWSLETTER

GET UPDATES,
FREEBIES & GIVEAWAYS

RENEEJOINERAUTHOR.COM/NEWSLETTER

Chapter One

Her blood was darker than she'd expected. It was hotter, thicker. Like someone had put it in a pot and boiled it. The blood made her dress cling to her body, and Alaina watched as the hot liquid stained the fabric. Her heart was breaking. She could tell by the silence in her chest, the emptiness in her stomach. The shattered pieces of the organ beat in her throat. It was begging to get out, even if it had to crawl its way out her mouth. It was willing to do anything to get away from the iron maiden that was her body, destroying everything inside of her. An otherworldly chanting echoed through the vast space. It would have given her the chills, were she not already cold to the bone. Those eyes were what caused the ice in her blood, the steel gray that stared her down as if she was nothing to him. She could almost hear her heartbreaking a little more.

Alaina fell to her knees, the pain in her body pushing and pulling her down. She could do nothing to fight it. Her mouth opened in a noiseless scream. Alaina couldn't find her voice. She knew she should have been happy about that; she didn't want to hear the pain in it, the despair and heartache. The blood trickling from the wound tickled her skin beneath her dress. It would have been pleasant, were it not for the knife protruding from her stomach. Her fingers danced over it gingerly. Even in this state of mind, she knew that pulling the knife out would be fatal. She would bleed out. Still, she was tempted to do so. She wanted the misery to end, but she couldn't bring herself to do it. Instead, she watched as the filament of energy arced around him, his emotionless face still harder than the ground she was trying to get up from. The energy was bright around him, the fuzzy darkness only blurring the edges ever so slightly.

There was now an ethereal glow beneath the gray of his eyes.

She felt a tugging at her energy. Alaina didn't have to look around to see who was so violently fighting against her. She was getting tired, and Zachariah was winning. She was certain every ounce of energy she had was getting ripped from her soul. It was painful. It was oh, so painful.

Alaina closed her eyes, her lids heavy, and her chest tight. She was struggling to breathe now. Somehow, the missing energy had taken her breath with it. The air seemed odd. Felt as thick as her blood, the sticky liquid that still oozed from the wound like a red waterfall. Alaina shivered as a new wave of ice followed the blood. It was so cold, nearly burning her skin. This was it; she was going to die. She was going to die with a broken heart, cold and shivering, with her energy being drained little by little. Soon enough, there would be nothing left.

All the remaining power in her limbs started to fade. She imagined the cold in her bones as a demon, chasing away the energy with its sharp teeth and cruel smile. The world tilted, moving too fast for her to keep up. Bile rose in her throat, but it made her feel weightless. She preferred that feeling over the throbbing in her limbs, her stomach. Alaina's head rolled back, and her body fought against the encroaching darkness. There wasn't much she could do. There was no way for her weak body to fight against the cold, the darkness, the exhaustion. Under normal circumstances, maybe, but with a broken, shattered heart, it was much more difficult.

Alaina didn't know she was falling until her body hit the ground. She felt the impact vibrate through her bones. Alaina couldn't get back up. She couldn't move her limbs to even get into a more comfortable position. Alaina just stayed there, her body bent in unnatural directions, looking at the stone archways high above her. She tried to focus on the patterns, the cracks. But they all faded into one another. Her vision swam, and the archways started to fade. She tried to hold on to them. Tried, but failed...

She knew she had to fight. She had to fight these people. But how could she when she was all alone, overpowered and outnumbered? How could she when there was nothing left for her to fight for? No, that was a lie. There was plenty to fight for. Her sisters, her friends, her world. This world that would fall to the likes of Zachariah. She couldn't allow that to happen. She loved this world too much, even if it was a cruel and unforgiving place to her kind. She believed that one day the witches would be accepted, but until then, she had to preserve this world. She had to protect it. Every mortal would be killed if Zachariah had his way, and she couldn't allow it. She had to fight.

Fight.

Alaina felt her magic at her fingertips, felt the weak pulsing in her veins. Could she fight this? Could she really get up and face them in this state? No. She was hopeful, but not stupid. She knew her only chance was escaping.

The stone beneath her fingers was hot compared to her skin. Her fingernails broke as she clawed at it, splitting and bleeding. Good. The more blood, the better. She couldn't feel the tips of her fingers anymore, anyway. Blood was the best medium to do spells with. This was good.

In the distance, she could hear voices. They were angry, demanding things. She couldn't hear what it was, but she knew that voice and that voice never asked, only ordered. Brenna, her sister. She was here. And wherever Brenna was, Morgan was close behind. She wanted to call out to them. To tell them not to trust these men, but she couldn't. She needed all her strength to fight the tugging at her mind that battled for control. No, she had to fight that tug. She held on like the stubborn witch she was, chanting her words of power. Each word she whispered returned another tendril of strength to her body. It wasn't much, but each tendril made her whisper, louder, louder until it wasn't a whisper anymore. Just a little more. She just had to fight a little longer, get a bit more power.

A shadow loomed over her. It forced the blurry, cracked stones of the archways out of her sight, demanding her full attention. His face was set in a sneer. He was angry, he was disgusted, and he was just too familiar. Those emerald eyes would haunt her for the rest of her time on this earth and the next. The eyes of a traitor…

Alaina's heart pounded in her throat, and she could feel the power slowly slipping away from her again. There was a mewl of pain, and she only realized after that it had come from her. Her body exploded in agony. Her fingertips, her stomach, her heart, her veins, from the lack of magic in them.

Fight.

Anger rippled through her, causing a jolt of resistant magic to course along with the link. She felt her captor recoil, and the face above her contorted in… something. Surprise? Alaina couldn't quite place the emotion. Her body stopped shivering as her numbing fingers continuously traced patterns with her blood on the stone.

"Give in to him, Alaina."

His voice was commanding in a way she had never heard it before. Her heart ached for her loss, and she felt her power being drained. Alaina fought to regain control. A dull tugging in her abdomen made her look down. His hand was wrapped around the blade, pressing it deeper into her. It didn't hurt, not any more than it already did. She felt the edge tremble and vibrate as the tip met the resistance of bone. Alaina watched, helpless as he slowly twisted it. The pain flared into something more acute than the dull throb.

She choked on the growing fear and pain, and her whispers stopped. Her lips parted in a voiceless scream, replaced by a soft gurgle. Alaina swallowed, and then swallowed again, tasting metal. Her voice barely a whisper now, Alaina drew more of her power back from him, letting it fill her like soap bubbles. It was weak and still weakening, but it was all Alaina had left. Tracing more complex patterns in her blood, Alaina held on to her strength with all her might, focusing on the words of power that would set the spell in motion.

"Give in," Damon sneered, his eyes bright with malice and barely contained anger.

Alaina's vision darkened as he jerked the blade from her stomach, and her chant faltered. Her blood felt impossibly hot, burning her skin as it poured from the wound. She watched as Damon stepped away from her, the blade dripping darkly onto the stone.

"Give in, Alaina."

Alaina reached toward him, and he laughed, cold and

high. Her breathing became shallow, raspy. She was dying, and she knew it.

Fight!

Closing her eyes, Alaina concentrated hard on the sensation of the stone beneath her fingers. It was the only thing keeping her conscious as she completed the series of symbols drawn in her own blood. If she could just...

Her eyes flew open as she felt Zachariah yank hard at the hold he had over her mind and her magic, strengthening the tendrils of energy that flowed from her to him. Alaina felt her magic drain out of her like water flows from a jug, powerless to resist. Desperate, she clung to the words of power in her mind, too weak to move her lips and give voice to them. She repeated them over and over, using them as an anchor, unable to move anymore.

Alaina didn't remember closing her eyes again, but everything around her was dark. She felt her breath rattle in her throat as her chest labored to draw in more of the stale, thick air. She could hear Zachariah still chanting as the last of her power evaporated. The separation felt like pressure in her head.

She had expected more from her death. A clamor of drums, or trumpets, but not the complete silence that fell. She could no longer feel or hear or smell. Alaina exhaled, or at least, she thought she did. She exhaled and gave in to the darkness, wanting nothing more than to rest.

Fight!

△▽△

ALAINA OPENED her eyes to the sound of a strange beeping noise. She didn't recognize it, but somehow, she knew what it was. Her fingers twitched as she tried to move them. She had to cover her eyes. The light was too bright, too white. Everything was too white. She inhaled; the smell of the room was different somehow. She flinched. Her body ached. Her head hurt, too, the pressure in her skull too much for her to endure. Alaina choked on a sob. Was this purgatory? Was she dead and cursed to this world of eternal suffering? No, she was alive. She knew it. She had to be. This wasn't the purgatory that she'd read about in the tomes. No, this was too real. There were no illusions to torment her, no inky blackness to envelop her. She was alive, and she was breathing. The only difference was that she didn't recognize the room she woke up in.

The ceiling looked wrong. The room looked wrong. Everything looked wrong. It was too bright and too loud. Alaina searched her memory, but the pain drew her back to the present. She closed her eyes. An image of a blinding light and a piercing scream flashed through her.

A car crash, her brain enlightened her. She remembered an argument with a man she didn't recognize. "Noah," her mind seemed to say. Yes, Noah was his name. They had argued about something silly. She couldn't remember what it was. There was a blinding light and then...

A crash. Alaina watched from the outside now. She watched as medics rushed a lifeless woman's body to an odd-looking box. No, that was an ambulance. She didn't know how she knew the name of the object, but she did. She knew what they were doing. She floated above them all, following the ambulance to the hospital.

Her heart thumped hard in her chest, shaking her, bringing her crashing down, down, down. Or, perhaps, she was already shaking. Alaina frowned. She knew it wasn't her own memory, but it had felt real. The incessant beeping drew her attention, and Alaina squinted at the contraption. "Heart monitor," her brain offered. She was connected to a heart monitor.

"No," Alaina whispered, "this is wrong. I didn't…"

She sat up, her hand automatically going to her stomach. Alaina's eyes widened as her memory came flooding back. Damon standing there, dagger dripping blood… Cold gray eyes that could pierce a brick wall with one look. She remembered tugging, she remembered blood. She remembered a stone hall that was once a meeting point for the coven. By the time she'd gotten there, Zachariah had already converted it to his own chamber of horrors. It was no longer a safe place for witches. No, he'd made sure of that. There was one image that stuck in her head, though. A dagger, her abdomen, a cruel smile.

Alaina hurriedly yanked the sheet from her body, pulling the wires that connected to her arms off with it. An alarming sound came from the machine, but she ignored it. She couldn't focus on anything. There was no time to examine her surroundings. There was no time to assess where she was. The material. She had to get it out of the way as soon as possible. She had to see something. She had to look. How had she survived? Alaina hastily tugged her garment up over her belly.

She stared at her abdomen. The gauze was clean and wrapped stiffly around her middle. Tears choked her, blurring her vision.

How am I alive?

Shakily, Alaina fumbled with the gauze. She needed to see, needed to be sure. Her numb fingers couldn't entirely complete the task, and it made her clench her teeth in frustration as she tugged clumsily at the tape. Alaina felt no pain.

At the sound of a commotion outside the door, her head shot up. She could see people moving outside, shadows hastily scurrying to get to her. Alaina swallowed. She hardly even noticed the gauze turning crimson under her probing fingers. Someone burst through the door. "A nurse," her mind said. Then, there was another person, a man this time. She recognized his face, but it took a moment to place him. Wasn't he the man in the car with her? The man she'd had the argument with. His face was contorted in panic, but when he saw her, it was replaced with relief.

"Lindsey," he mumbled as if his eyes were deceiving him. She could make out the lines of worry. The name was familiar, but it also felt wrong.

With gentle hands, the nurse forced her down onto the bed. From distant memory, she knew that it was better to do as the nurse said than to fight it. The nurse was talking, but Alaina did not hear. Her ears were still ringing, and her body was shaking. Too scared to close her eyes, Alaina simply stared at the man. Somehow, he anchored her to the present. Her mind stopped its frantic aimless and meaningless babbling. This strange man seemed to know who she was.

She saw guilt in his eyes, overpowering the relief. It was heartbreaking.

"Lindsey," he mumbled again, but then he was ushered out of the room, and the door closed behind him.

The nurse removed Alaina's bandages, and she felt a faint tugging as the woman mended her wound. Alaina glanced down at the nurse's nimble fingers. She saw the dark knit of stitches and blood where Alaina had reopened her wound. It ran from her navel to her breastbone, held together by thin black thread. The injury was still red around the edges and angrier now that she had accidentally torn it open. Damon had stabbed her. No, she reminded herself, he had gutted her. She could still feel the blade, as though it was nevertheless plunged inside of her, the icy tip still scraping against bone. Alaina suppressed a shiver.

"Now, don't go fiddling with your bandages again. You've had a terrible ordeal, and you need to rest. The doctor should be by shortly to check up on you."

This was the first time Alaina had actually heard the woman speak. She had a kind voice, the sort that demanded trust and love. Her gentle, brown eyes matched her voice, and her mouse-brown hair was pulled into a tight bun on top of her head. She looked older than Alaina, but somehow Alaina knew that she was far, far older than this woman.

Alaina nodded at the kind woman who patted her hand and left. The door opened, and she saw the man waiting just outside, pressing the nurse for information. The nurse allowed him to enter her room, and Alaina watched as he approached the bed, much like a young child would approach their mother after they had broken her vase. Alaina felt a vague tugging of recognition, but it was gone like a wisp of smoke. Who was this man to her?

"How do you feel?" he asked.

"I'm not sure," Alaina admitted. She looked at the needle in her arm, aware now that it supplied the morphine that dulled her pain. No doubt, it also added to the floating feeling in her head.

"Lindsay, I..."

Alaina, suddenly annoyed at the disorientation and the fear of being in an unfamiliar place, glared at him. "That isn't my name."

The bewilderment on his face was nearly enough to make her laugh, but she felt no humor in her current state. Her voice still sounded the same to her; her body always felt the same, even if it did feel weaker. It felt a lot more vulnerable if she was honest, but she felt the same. She was still Alaina. She didn't understand why everything felt so terribly wrong.

She knew she wasn't at the right time. And yet, despite the disorientation, Alaina felt as if she had always known this place.

"You don't remember." It was a statement rather than a question. "Do you know who I am?"

Alaina shook her head. "Noah," her mind said, but she ignored it. Knowing a person's name didn't mean she knew who he was.

His face paled, and for the first time, Alaina saw the scratches and bruises. She could tell that his nose had been broken recently, and the hand he pushed through his hair had a bandage around the wrist. The left side of his face was purple. It reminded her of the time Damon punched his brother. Only, this purple shade wasn't restricted to his eye. No, this covered the whole side of his face. He must have been beaten up quite severely... Or, no. He had been in a car crash.

"Who are you?" Alaina asked, a gnawing uncertainty in her stomach.

"Noah," he said simply, though there were some under-lying emotions in his voice. Alaina couldn't put the finger on it, and she didn't have the time to care. She had to figure out what was going on.

A sharp knock had both of them start and face the door. A tall man in a white coat walked in, holding a...

Alaina squinted at the object in his hand. "Clipboard," her mind helped her. He had a clipboard in his hand. Alaina furrowed her brows at him as he flipped through the pages.

"Lindsey, your nurse Elise informs me that you had

an," the doctor paused, "episode when you woke up." He set the clipboard down and approached her.

"Episode?" Alaina's voice came out harsher than she had expected. The word rankled her. It brought to mind accusations of madness.

"I didn't have an episode," she said, stressing the word, aware that there was a sudden rise in pitch in her voice. "I woke up in a strange place, connected to machines and, and these pipes…"

She shook her arm, making the tubes tinkle lightly against the bed frame. Alaina's voice broke. "I was alone."

"Doctor, she doesn't remember what happened to her," Noah offered meekly.

The doctor contemplated Alaina's reddening face as she struggled to maintain her composure. He took a deep breath before speaking. "You woke up alone and afraid. It is understandable, then, that you reacted the way you did."

There was a fire in her stomach. She wanted to tell him that he was damn right, it was perfectly normal, but then she realized that there was nothing normal about this.

The doctor returned to the clipboard and made a few notes. Occasionally, he looked up at the monitor and noted that information down, too.

"I understand that this must be quite unsettling for you, but don't worry. You'll feel like yourself again in no time."

He proceeded to run a few tests, alternating between checking whatever it was that needed checking and writing notes. Alaina wanted to grab the clipboard and beat him with it. How could he be so calm? She was losing her mind. Alaina fought the urge to make a scene. It didn't matter who she was or where she was, if she was alive, so were Damon and Zachariah. Alaina had to keep quiet and stay out of as much trouble as possible. At least until she could figure out what was going on.

"Amnesia is quite common for people who have been in serious car accidents," the doctor said, sounding aloof.

"A car accident?" Alaina asked just as the memory flashed through her mind. "I think I remember." Her brows furrowed as she recalled the incident. "There were lights and screaming. And then there was pain and darkness."

The doctor caught Alaina's eye, and she watched him scribble something down after checking her pupil responses. The doctor smiled reassuringly. "There doesn't seem to be permanent damage, but I would like to double-check. I'll schedule an MRI."

Alaina's mind raced for an explanation.

"It's basically a brain scan that allows us to monitor blood flow and functionality," her own voice told her, inside her head.

"Why?" she asked the doctor out loud.

"You were in a coma, while you are awake now, you might not be completely out of the woods yet. It will ensure that we don't miss anything," he explained patiently.

"I'm so sorry, Lindsey," Noah said before Alaina could ask the doctor more questions. She looked at him, wondering where that guilt on his face was coming from. He'd been driving, she remembered. He was blaming himself for the accident?

"The memories will come in short bursts. It may take a while before you remember everything, but don't worry too much about it," the doctor assured her.

After a few more tests and more reassurances, the doctor left Alaina and Noah alone for a moment. Alaina was still shaking slightly and had balled her fists to keep her hands steady. Her body trembled as her body adjusted to the sensory overload.

"You really don't remember me?" Noah asked quietly.

Alaina looked at him and searched Lindsey's broken memories but came up blank. She shook her head and sighed. "No."

Noah managed to keep himself in check, something Alaina would give him credit for. "There's no rush. Get some rest, okay?"

Alaina felt a phantom pain of rejection as her memories danced around Damon. She had loved once, and it had gotten her killed.

"Thank you," Alaina said as he stood to leave, "for trying."

Both Noah and Lindsey were innocent bystanders in this messed-up situation, and she felt terrible for him. Lindsay was gone, and yet with Alaina alive, she was giving him hope that his Lindsey would come back to him.

He simply smiled.

After Noah had left her room, Alaina closed her eyes and forced herself to relive her last moments. She saw Damon as he dropped the mask, his smile dissolving into a sneer seconds before Zachariah plunged the blade into her soft body. She remembered how it burned as the length of it was forced through her flesh. She remembered how it squelched wetly.

Alaina inhaled deeply, grateful that she was able to do so without struggling.

"It wasn't a dream."

Alaina was comforted by that fact. It also meant that somehow, she had survived. Alaina could still feel her power which meant...

She hastily shoved the thought away, but she knew.

They had failed.

But what she couldn't understand was this: Damon had

betrayed the coven, and he had betrayed her, trading her life and her power for... for what? More power?

Despite the relief she felt for their failure, she couldn't get this thought out of her head. It didn't matter how hard she tried. It circled in her mind, the look on his face seared into her memory. His gray eyes, his cold sneer, his cruel smile...

Anger welled in her stomach and took over her body, drowning every other emotion. It felt like a tsunami, wave after wave of merciless rage. Alaina felt a spark in her fingertips. Her magic was slowly stirring back to life, back to its former glory. The tsunami of anger died down as she stretched her limbs, letting the magic snake its way through her veins, letting it go wherever it wanted. She had her magic to thank for her life. It could do whatever it wanted if it was up to her. Her next breath was sweet as if she had been holding her breath this entire time. The first breath after holding it for an extended period was always the most delicious.

Uninvitedly, Alaina's mind dashed toward Lindsay's life.

Lindsay, the girl she was meant to be. The girl whose body she was possessing, the girl who had a man who loved her, who had a life, the girl who'd died a terrible death.

Alaina skipped through her memories, trying to find anything tangible or worth making sense of. They were all torn and spread apart. Some memories were missing endings, some beginnings, and some only consisted of a beginning and an end. There was nobody to these memories. Alaina huffed in frustration. The only useful thing in this woman's head was the names of things. She could look around the room and name every single object, even though she had never seen these things before in her life. The technology was far too advanced for her time, yet these things seemed no stranger to her than a wood-burning stove.

With sudden clarity, Alaina realized that her spell had worked. As a last-ditch effort to destroy the ritual, she had tied herself to Zachariah. He had taken her power of his own free will, and so she'd allowed the binding to happen. One moment, she was dying on the cold, stone floor, and the next, she woke up 300 years later.

Alaina sank into the soft pillow, sighing with relief. Time did not overlook witches and warlocks, which meant Zachariah should be dead, and so should the traitor who'd told her he loved her. But no...

Alaina opened her eyes, gasping. She had tied herself to Zachariah. If she was alive, he had to be as well. She'd tied their life forces together to take him down with her. But if she was still alive, that meant that Zachariah was still at large, and she was in a hospital bed, breathing in the cleaning chemicals and trying to make sense of her new world.

She had to get out of there. She had to find Zachariah and put an end to him once and for all.

△▽△

ALAINA FELL INTO A DRUG-INDUCED SLEEP, grateful for the dreamlessness that came with it. When she awoke, Noah was at her side, his head rolled back and his mouth slightly open with sleep.

Another quick flash of memory allowed her a glimpse of Lindsey's past. Noah was asleep in much the same position while the flickering light of the television played across his features. A smile played on her lips as she watched him, her own memories stirring up afterimages of love. Alaina stifled the memory in disgust, shoving thoughts of Damon away from her.

"Traitor."

"What?" It wasn't until Noah looked at her through a sleepy haze that she realized she had spoken the word aloud.

Alaina shook her head. "It's nothing."

"I didn't mean to wake you," she added, too aware of the fact that he saw Lindsey instead of her. Noah's answering smile made her heart ached. Alaina squashed down her feelings and adjusted her position in bed.

"The doctor says that you can come home today, Lindsey." His face was bright, even through the dark circles of sleeplessness.

"Noah, I…" Alaina started just as a nurse interrupted them. Her gaze flickered to him, and her throat went dry.

Damon.

She was all too grateful that the infernal beeping machine was no longer connected to her. In essence, it would have only served to alert him of her rapidly beating heart.

It couldn't be. And yet it was. There was no mistaking the dark hair and the steely gray eyes. A whirlwind of emotion stirred up inside of her.

Longing, joy, anger, and despair, all blending into one massive, indigestible ball of acid and pain.

The nurse looked at her with a practiced smile. "Doc has given you the all-clear, Lindsay. We just need you to sign this before we can let you go."

Damon placed the form in front of her on her bed tray and waited.

He is watching you, Alaina.

Alaina forced a smile of relief and gratitude. "That's

super," she said and grabbed the pen, surprised that her hands weren't giving her away.

Noah's joy bled from his every pore as he recognized Lindsey in the way Alaina spoke and moved her body.

Fight!

Alaina struggled for control to keep the smile in place. If Damon knew who she really was, he didn't let on. She happily signed the release papers and handed the pen back to Damon without breaking her composure.

"Well, there you go. Just need to finalize some things and you're ready to go. If you could follow me, please, Mr. Grant." Damon gathered the form and headed for the door. Alaina's heart still beat frantically against her ribs.

After giving her a reassuring smile, Noah followed after Damon.

Chapter Two

ALAINA SWALLOWED HARD AROUND A LUMP IN HER THROAT that wasn't there a moment ago.

How was this even possible? How was he still alive? Alaina did the math in her head. The last date in Lindsey's memory was in the 21st century. This meant that over 300 years had passed. It was impossible that Damon was still alive. It made sense if it were Zachariah, but Damon? No, there must be an explanation.

Alaina forced herself to remain calm, needing to focus. She needed to put up a ward spell to keep Damon oblivious to her true identity. If he didn't already know that this poor, damaged girl was actually Alaina, then the ward would keep him from looking too hard at her. At least until she managed to get out of the hospital.

And if he already knew who she was…

Well, the ward would, at the very least, keep him from tracking her magic. It was the only thing she could do in her weakened state, and she hoped it would be enough. She felt the familiar tingle of magic as it wrapped itself around her mind and body. She was sluggish, but Alaina traced the symbols of power in the air, a faint ethereal glow trailing her fingertips, and murmured the words that accompanied them. With a soft whisper of wind, the ward was set.

It was strange how magic worked. Any sliver of magic could be traced by a skilled enough witch or warlock, but the simplest of wards could block them out entirely. Most witches didn't have the mind to put up protections, but Alaina always did. It didn't matter where she went or who she was with. She'd rather be safe than dead.

Alaina could only tell it was there because she had placed it and knew what to look for.

A phantom pain started in her abdomen where the blade had been, and Alaina gently rested her hand over the still-healing wound. While her other injuries had mostly healed, that one was taking longer than it should have.

Magical injuries always seemed to heal slower than the usual kind. Alaina wondered if the dagger had somehow acted as a conduit. If that was the case, then it would be reasonable to assume that Damon had unknowingly imparted some of his own magic into her when he had stabbed her.

Alaina sighed unhappily.

She sat upright in the bed when the pain finally subsided. Alaina thought back and remembered her thin mattress on the farm. No, beds hadn't come very far, if this stupid hospital bed was anything to go by. Her back hurt from lying on the mattress for so long. She couldn't wait to get up and taste life again, to get back on her feet. She hated being vulnerable. She hated needing someone to take care of her. But like her gran had once told her, "If you need help to get back on your feet, take it. It will go faster than trying to do it yourself."

The woman's wise words still stuck in Alaina's head.

This didn't mean that she had to be lying down all day long. There was the possibility that she wasn't going 'home' just yet, but if she was going to take down Zachariah and Damon, she had to get back to her full strength as soon as possible. Home. The word left a bitter taste in her mouth. It wasn't her home. It was the home of the body she inhabited.

"Lindsey?"

Alaina looked guiltily at the doorway, where Noah had appeared.

"What are you doing?"

Her mouth went dry. This was silly. Noah didn't know what she was thinking about another person's home, so he must have been commenting on her upright position.

"I…" Alaina couldn't immediately think of a response. She wanted to tell him off for being too overprotective and kind, but she knew there was a reason Lindsey had chosen him. Realizing that the only way she would be able to maintain her cover was to play along; Alaina drew on Lindsey's memories. To remain undetected, Alaina had to become Lindsey. She had to become a dead girl and pretend to be alive.

Alaina breathed in as if inhaling Lindsey.

She tucked her hair behind her ear as if Lindsey's muscles remembered precisely what this body should be doing when it felt shy.

"I wanted to…" Her voice broke slightly, and she cleared her throat. She wasn't sure if this was fake or real. It felt authentic. "I have to use the…" Alaina pointed toward the little bathroom attached to her room.

Noah frowned at her before his face flushed red. He rushed over and offered her his arm. "Sorry. Let me help you."

Knowing that this fragile body was still too weak,

Alaina accepted the offered arm and leaned her weight on him as she slid from the bed. It felt strange, being on her feet again. The floor felt bizarre beneath her bare feet. She looked down at her toes. She could tell they had once been painted red, but the polish was slowly chipping away. She could hear Lindsey's voice saying that she needed to patch it up when she got home. What an odd thing to do.

Alaina was grateful to put her weight on Noah's arm. Every joint, limb, and muscle ached as she tried to walk. Lindsey was only in a coma for a couple of weeks. Still, the inactivity had clearly taken a toll on the woman's body. Not to mention the injuries that this body had suffered.

Nevertheless, even after all of that, this body felt too weak, too soft. This body was much more delicate than Alaina's. Alaina had been strong. Stronger than many girls her age, working in the fields with her father and mother, collecting and chopping wood for the icy winters. Even after all of that, her body wouldn't have turned to this state. Lindsey's body wasn't used to manual labor, she could tell that much.

Alaina suppressed her irritation and anger when she had to stop to catch her breath after only a few steps. Beads of sweat had begun to form at her hairline and at the nape of her neck.

"It's okay, Lindy," Noah said encouragingly.

She didn't have to look at him to know that he was smiling an infuriatingly reassuring smile. He was too kind, too nice. Her memories flooded with Damon. He had once pretended to be kind, also. But he'd only done it to get close to her. He'd only done it to make her fall in love with him, only to break her heart as he plunged a dagger in her.

"The doctor said that your body should recover soon," Noah added. "You'll get stronger again."

Alaina wanted to tell him that he was talking rubbish.

She wanted to say to him that this body was weak to begin with, that there was no time for "eventually." The threat was here now. Zachariah and Damon were at large now. There was no time to get stronger. She had to make do with what she had, and what she had was frustrating.

Knowing she had to bite her tongue, Alaina didn't speak until she came to the bathroom. "Thank you," she mumbled, using the wall to support herself as she closed the bathroom door behind her.

Alaina sat down on the closed lid of the toilet, staring at herself in the large mirror. She didn't look like herself anymore. Gone was her corn-colored braid that made few women envious and her eyes the color of ice. Her blue eyes always had been her most dominant feature. It was the thing everyone saw first, and the thing everyone seemed to talk about afterward. But Alaina's soft features had been replaced by Lindsey's. These features were sharper. Lindsey had the sort of face that would make anyone stop in their tracks. For a moment, she wondered if Lindsey had any help keeping her hair so black. Alaina remembered the girls in her village using berries to turn their hair red. Somehow, she doubted Lindsey was the type to waste her time and efforts on such things. Besides, her hair was too thick and healthy. There was no way it would look this radiant after being subjected to harsh chemical treatments. Alaina was initially confused by the thought, but quickly realized it was Lindsey's mind defending herself. Alaina grinned. This was going to be one hell of an adventure.

She stared Lindsey's reflection in the eyes. As striking as Alaina's blue eyes were, so were Lindsey's green ones. They looked supernatural as if she was half cat. Or perhaps, Alaina gasped, a witch. It would explain her flawless, porcelain skin, her eyes, and her hair. There was nothing ordinary about this woman.

Alaina inspected Lindsey's hair once more. She wasn't used to having such a mop. Lifting thick bangs that were a little too long, she revealed some fresh scars. They were brutal looking, and she arranged the hair over her forehead to hide it once again. The face frowned at her, and she wanted to toss a toilet paper roll at the mirror. This face that was not her own infuriated her. It didn't matter how beautiful she was, it was not her face. Alaina reminded herself that she was in this body because they shared similar injuries that caused their deaths. They were both gutted because of the people they loved. Lindsey's face softened a bit. They were two of a kind, though Alaina doubted Noah was as responsible for Lindsey's death as Damon was for hers. Still, Alaina clung to the small connection.

When Alaina decided that she had wasted enough time staring at herself, she flushed the toilet and walked toward the sink. She didn't think twice about the flushing water behind her, but when she opened the tap, she marveled at how easy it was for the water to be obtained. The water was cool on her face as she splashed herself, comforting the cuts with a cold touch. She patted her face with a dry towel, taking extra care to avoid her injuries. She once again found herself looking at the scar beneath her fringe. A memory flooded her mind. Screeching tires as the car fought to slow. Her head hit the passenger side window, and Alaina grimaced. She could feel the wound throbbing as if to confirm the memory. Something like that would have killed a person back in Alaina's own time. But this wasn't what killed Lindsey, no. It was the gutting of her abdomen that had killed her. Alaina didn't even try to remember what happened. She could recall her own gutting just fine.

The memory came anyway. Alaina squeezed her eyes

shut, her heart hammering, as the thoughts assailed her. She could feel her wound pulse beneath the gauze in response. The car had hit the side of an oncoming truck, skidded, and rolled over the barrier, taking the metal supports with it.

When the vehicle finally came to a rest at the bottom of a small incline, she saw only the metal bar piercing the spider webbed windshield like a straw through the hole of a juice box.

Alaina blinked, and the memory was gone. She was surprised and completely unnerved by the intensity of Lindsey's memories. It was one thing to relive her own death, but having to relive the death of another in such vivid detail... It was horrifying, like nothing she had ever seen in her life. It was gruesome and awful, too much for her weak heart to bear. This girl, this poor girl, had done nothing to deserve such an end but had gotten it anyway. Just like Alaina didn't deserve her own end. She felt a stronger connection to Lindsey. Somehow, she knew that Lindsey and she would have been great friends in another time. After splashing more water on her face, she returned to Noah and let him help her back into bed.

△▽△

THERE WERE few things as comforting as sleep. Rest was the best way to recover, after all. When she returned from the bathroom, Alaina fell back asleep. She didn't know how much time had passed before she woke up again, but she saw that the sun was beginning to set outside her window. She was feeling a lot better, but there was still a weakness in her bones. She hated it.

Alaina sat up in her bed, finding Noah in a chair next to her, the chair he had sunken into after he'd helped her back to her bed earlier that morning. There was a gym bag at his feet. Lindsey's. Did this mean she was being released? Did this mean she was finally going home, away from Damon? She hoped so.

A memory of a soft bed forced itself into her mind, the feeling of wrapping herself in warm sheets. Alaina grinned. That was one of Lindsey's memories. She was delighted to test out.

Alaina watched Noah. He hadn't noticed her yet, and she was grateful for it. His constant presence was tiring, but she had no doubt that it was the reason why Damon hadn't investigated further. She now examined the man who shielded her from her horrible past, watching as his eyebrows creased in concentration. He was reading an old paperback that he had folded in half. She could feel the remnants of what was left of Lindsey's mind recoil at the site. She'd always hated the way he abused books.

Despite the somewhat psychotic nature of his abuse toward the poor book, Alaina could see why Lindsey was so infatuated with him. He had sun-kissed skin that seemed a little faded. Probably from sitting inside all the time, babysitting Lindsey. His eyes were like two midnight skies, sparkling with stars. He had a strong face, the sort she used to fawn over in her old life. His mop of dark brown hair was thick enough to match Lindsey's. Alaina couldn't help but wonder what their kids would've looked like. Lindsey's eyes and his strong brow, a head of hair that looked wig-like. Alaina shook the thought from her head. It was obviously something Lindsey thought of frequently.

"You know," Alaina rasped, sitting upright with a cringe. Her throat was dry, and she reached for the glass of water on her nightstand. "You really shouldn't abuse a book like that."

Noah's head shot up, his full lips twisted with amusement. He shrugged. "Your grandmother once told me that men who abuse books get punished by the gods in the afterlife."

Alaina chuckled. "And you're willing to risk the wrath of the gods?"

Another smile from Noah and Lindsey's stomach turned. "I like to keep things interesting. Who wants a boring afterlife anyway?"

The water was still cold as she drank. Noah must have filled it up for her a few minutes before she woke up. Alaina peered at him, curiously over the edge of the cup. She could feel the remnants of Lindsey's love flicker in her chest. This was going to take some getting used to. Her mind was clearer now, and she could quickly flip through her own memories, struggling less with Lindsey's. The girl's brain had taken a substantial hit during her accident, and some of her memories were still hazy, if not completely inaccessible. Yet, there were things in Lindsey's mind that completely overpowered Alaina's own. Her love for Noah, their cat called Salem that had died a year after they'd gotten it, her grandmother who had passed away only a few months after Lindsey's mother. Lindsey was sure that it was due to a broken heart. Losing her only child had aged Lindsey's grandmother overnight. There were things that even a broken mind could never forget, Alaina realized. No matter how hard one might try.

"Have you been sitting here all day?" Alaina asked as she glanced at the darkening sky outside the window once again.

"I went home to change and clean up a bit before you come home..." He trailed off and cleared his throat. "Anyway, the doc says you can go home today. Your injuries are healing up pretty fast now."

Alaina tried to remember their home but couldn't put a

finger on it. It made her nervous. She didn't like going into things blindly. Still, Alaina couldn't help but smile; she was looking forward to the freedom the outside world offered.

△▽△

ALAINA WISHED she had stayed dead as they walked up the fourth flight of stairs. Noah helped her as much as he could, but considering her injuries, it was still a painful task. It took well over 20 minutes to get Alaina's broken body up the stairs, and she was growing increasingly impatient with Noah as well. Who did he think he was anyway? Telling her where to step and how to breathe? Was he the one who was gutted like a pig? Was he the one in another body? He didn't know anything. He didn't know a damned thing.

Alaina quickly pushed away her annoyance. This wasn't going to help anyone. It wasn't his fault that she was a strange woman in an unknown time. She was to blame for that. It was her fault, with her stupid spells and the stupid traitors that forced her to cast them. Everything was stupid. The stairs, the railing, Noah's hands on her body, Noah's encouragement, and especially Alaina's mind, for being angry at the poor man when he had lost the love of his life and now had to take care of an imposter.

Alaina swallowed every bit of anger and irritation. Years of studying witchcraft had told her that nothing good ever came from being angry or in love. Those were the two things that made people stupid, and Alaina couldn't afford to be stupid. She couldn't afford the mistakes she was bound to make. There was a greater evil in the world, and she was the only person who knew how to stop it. Unless some other witch had risen in the 300 years that she had missed who knew the forbidden spells, the dark, dangerous ones that no one dared mention. She doubted it. She had burned a good number of tomes after reading them. There were only a few in existence.

Sensing Alaina's impatience, Noah made haste to shove the key in the keyhole. The door was plain, nothing special about it. It did look a little run-down, but it was still the best looking door on the floor. Alaina looked around, and a vision popped into her head. It was Lindsey, scrubbing the door and giving it a fresh layer of paint. The landlord had refused to fix it. He'd said something about it not being an inconvenience to them and so it was not his responsibility. Lindsey was so angry that she'd scrubbed the door with a toothbrush before painting it a bright red. She'd wanted to make a point, and she had. It stood out in the crowd of dull blue doors. The landlord wasn't happy but never bothered changing it back to the sickly blue.

Alaina was vaguely aware that Noah was talking to her. She looked at him in confusion.

"What?"

"The accident," Noah said, rubbing the back of his neck. "It was my fault. It's my fault that you can't remember. It's my fault we got into that accident. I was driving."

Alaina's heart tightened. "We don't have to talk about this now."

Noah opened the door, revealing a small, cramped apartment that seemed both strange and familiar. The sensation made Alaina's head spin, and she used the wall to support herself as she stepped inside. Her attention was torn in half. One half on Noah, and the other on the apartment. It was tidy and clean. It smelled like home. Alaina couldn't quite place what it was. It was citrusy, but there was an underlying hint of something else. The walls were painted beige, and she could tell where photo frames were used to cover up the cracks or holes. She remembered how Noah had hung them, Lindsey lounging on the couch, telling him whether or not they were lopsided. Alaina smiled at the memory. It was one of the obvious ones.

The couches were oversized. Two people could comfortably sleep on one of them. They looked so comfortable.

"No, listen to me, Lindy," Noah started again.

Alaina peeked into the kitchen area. Brown wooden cupboards, a small stove, and oven, a large fridge. Alaina's stomach grumbled. She held a hand up, hoping it was enough to stop Noah from talking.

"Let's not talk about this now," she said as gently as she could. She didn't have the strength to go on about something that hadn't even happened to her. There was no time for it.

"Lindy, I need to talk about this and…"

"Stop!" Alaina's command hung in the air, suffocating them both. It was harsh, but it served its purpose.

Noah clenched his keys in his hand, and Alaina watched as his knuckles turned white. She didn't have the time or the energy right now to deal with him. He took her bag to the bedroom, and she followed quietly behind.

Lindsey had rarely seen Noah angry but knew what the silence meant. Alaina was now faced with the same silence. She would have to tread carefully if she wanted to get out of this place. She needed him if she was going to stay hidden.

"I cleaned up in here, it was a bit of a mess. I even did some laundry," Noah commented when he saw her gaping at the room.

"You never do laundry; you hate it," Alaina laughed lightly. Oh, how easily her memories came to her now. She saw the tension in his shoulders release. Noah placed her bag on the neatly made bed. Another thing that was far from normal. She recognized her small white laptop on a desk littered with textbooks and old paperbacks. It was in front of the window. She remembered that Lindsey had pushed the desk there so she could look out of the apartment to the world beyond. It made her feel free, her mind told her. The outlook made Lindsey feel more powerful than she actually was.

Alaina couldn't focus on that when there were more pressing matters. The laptop, she had to use it to find her sisters. If they had managed to survive 300 years, that was the machine that would find them. Alaina was confused as to what the laptop did, but knew that it would grant her access to anything she wanted to know.

Alaina's heart fluttered with hope. She had a way to find them…

"Lindsey," Noah started again.

"Noah," Alaina said, using Lindsey's words, "I know you need to talk about what you're feeling, but I'm still woozy from the pain meds, and I really don't feel well. Everything feels strange and different, and I just need to lie down for a bit."

There was a tense moment of silence as he digested her words.

"All right. Okay, sure. I'm sorry; I know you're still healing." Noah kissed her forehead, and she stiffened.

Whether he noticed or not, Alaina wasn't sure, because she couldn't make out the expression on his face when he finally turned to leave her to her own devices, closing the bedroom door behind him.

"Why do I feel guilty?" Alaina asked herself, forcing the emotion away.

She remained seated on the bed for a few moments, just taking in the room, inhaling the familiar yet strange scent. The bedding didn't match the drapes, but she remembered the vision that Lindsey had for this place. Little by little, they were going to fix it up. To make it a home. They never got that far.

"Time to get to work," Alaina muttered and sat herself down in front of the laptop at the cluttered desk. She entered the password through muscle memory. Allowing Lindsey's memories to supply names and information for everything she was looking at while her brain sifted through the information that she pulled up on the screen.

"Three hundred years," Alaina whispered the words to herself almost disbelievingly but realized that it made sense somehow. There was magic, dark, forbidden magic that could bring her sisters back, that is. If they had crossed over with her.

Morgan had always been the strongest of the three. It wasn't such a far-fetched thought that she could have found a way to follow Alaina into a new body. But Brenna? She wouldn't have dabbled in anything so dark.

Zachariah had had no such qualms and was no doubt still trying to complete his first mission. He had managed to convince Damon that the only way to real power was through him. Alaina gritted her teeth as an angry tear rolled down her cheek, and her wound throbbed once.

Alaina started pulling up information on her family tree. Information on the day she died, and the days that followed. She needed to know where her sisters had gone. Alaina's power was still too weak for her to feel them.

After hours of searching, Alaina came up empty-handed. Morgan had disappeared without a trace. Brenna had stayed in that sleepy little town for only a month after Alaina's death before she had boarded a sailing vessel and headed to the new world.

Alaina absently wondered if they had interred her bones.

She got to her feet and took a short walk around the room, looking at the various posters and shelved baubles that lined the walls. It was clear that Noah had occupied the space more frequently than Lindsey had. However, there were beginnings of cohabitation in the smaller, more delicate frames and knick-knacks that were placed sporadically through the room.

"They lived together," Alaina murmured, picking up the old teddy bear that Lindsey had saved from her childhood. The only memory she had of that time. On the bedside table was a small silver frame with a photo of Lindsey and another, older woman.

"Mom," her brain supplied.

She had died a year ago due to heart complications. Lindsey had had no other family that she'd cared to remember.

Alaina felt a pang of sadness, felt the loss and hollowness of being alone in a strange place without the strength and love of her sisters to guide her. She returned to the open page and decided to track the ship Brenna had boarded.

She found that Brenna had made it over to the Americas. She had lived a reasonably happy life in the south before traveling farther north; where she had died of old age. Alaina stared at the information until her eyes burned. The data was frustratingly insufficient, only stating that her ship might have docked farther south than what was on the manifest due to bad weather.

Alaina looked up the different port cities, thankful for the additional information Lindsey's studious brain had provided. Around the same time, Brenna traveled from South America to North America, two ships were headed north with several families and well-off individuals. One in

Virginia, the other in Louisiana. Alaina referenced a map and sat back, exhaling sharply.

"She's here somewhere."

Suddenly, it all made sense. Why she inhabited Lindsey's body. Why she was here. Her magic had taken her to a time and place where she could find her sisters so they could put a stop to Zachariah's plans. The power of three could change the world forever. The universe knew this, the spell she had cast knew this. The universe wanted her to find her sisters and, gods be damned, she would. The power nexus was close, too, she could feel it even in her weakened state. This was why she was resurrected here and not anywhere else in the world. The nexus was close, and that meant that Zachariah would be here, too. He relied on power, and 300 years ago, it was impossible to get to the nexus, but now, here... Alaina swallowed. It all made sense.

Morgan had gone into hiding, and Alaina was uncertain whether or not she was still alive. Brenna was here, buried somewhere in this state. If she couldn't track down Morgan, she had to raise Brenna. Brenna would know where Morgan had gone, and if she didn't, they could work together to find her. One witch's spells were not enough to track down someone who didn't want to be found. But two who shared blood... They would always find each other. Three was a complete number, and they couldn't be three if one was missing.

Fight!

It was time to find them and fight back.

Chapter Three

It had taken her a few days to get back into the routine of living with Noah. He'd made her breakfast each morning and helped her dress her wound, but her recovery was much too slow for comfort, and she wasn't sure if she had the juice to cast a spell strong enough to heal her.

It was the only wound on her body that was not fully healed, and Alaina felt that it was what had bound her to Lindsey's body in the first place. She didn't think that risking a spell would be worth dying a second time. Somehow, the accident had occurred at the same time that Zachariah had started drawing power from Alaina. The metal support bar of the barrier had penetrated Lindsey's body in the same spot, pinning her to the seat, forcing Lindsey to live through the same hell that Alaina had experienced as she'd bled out.

Alaina tucked her hair behind her ear as she pored over maps of Virginia and Louisiana, Lindsey's habit starting to find a permanent place in her own mannerisms. She had bound her hair in a braid to keep the curls from her face, but a stray strand or two had managed to escape.

Alaina wasn't used to having this much hair on her head. It was hard to keep it under control. She'd learned that she needed to wash her hair in a certain way to keep the curls from getting unruly. It was an effort every day she had to clean it.

Noah had offered up the bed for her, a gesture she was sure he was starting to regret. She recalled falling asleep on the couch once or twice, which had resulted in her whole body being twisted up in an uncomfortable and painful knot. Alaina smiled internally at the image of his tall frame, squashed onto the couch as he slept. Dark circles were forming under his eyes, and she knew those were there because she had avoided him as much as possible. Alaina had the unnerving feeling that he was starting to realize that she was no longer the woman he was in love with. She knew that the whole situation was stressful for him, but she couldn't be bothered to make an effort with Noah. She was going to die after this was all over, anyway, so she couldn't get attached to him. She couldn't risk him talking her out of whatever she had to do. Her life was still linked to Zachariah's, and if he died, so did she. There was no undoing it. And there was no other way to defeat him than to kill him once and for all.

A light tap on her door announced his entry. Noah stood in the doorway with a fresh cup of herbal tea. Her doctor had denied her the coffee that this body craved so much. She hated herbal tea. Alaina remembered that she used to love herbal tea back in her own time. She wanted it as if it were opium. But this body, this body that was not her own hated it, and Alaina started to taste the bitterness of the herbs that Lindsey hated so much. She had never tasted it before, and now, she couldn't think why she had enjoyed it so much.

"Can I come in?" Noah asked. Alaina did not miss the look of longing he gave the bed as she beckoned him in.

"Thank you."

An awkward silence fell, and Noah cleared his throat uneasily. "Lindsey, you know there are things we need to talk about." Alaina meant to cut him off, but he held up his hand and continued, "I want you to come with me. I want to show you something."

Alaina protested, "I had other plans today, Noah. I wanted to head into the city and get familiar with things again."

"You can still do that, Lindy. I'll drive you wherever you need to go. Please, just let me show you something."

Alaina examined the sharpness of his jaw; the look of despair in his eyes made her heart skip a beat. It was unlike him, Lindsey's memories told her. He was never one to be broken about anything. He hadn't seen his family in years, and he never seemed to miss them, but this... He was missing her and yet she was in the same room as him. She could tell he was confused by this. It made this strong man crumble. Noah was tougher, tougher than Lindsey ever was. He was strong and smart and mentally on another level. He was brilliant. This wasn't like anything Lindsey had ever seen in him, and it unsettled Alaina. She needed him to convince everyone around them that she had no idea who she was. And she needed to go along with it. If not to soothe Noah's aching heart, then for the sake of disguise.

Alaina reluctantly consented, and surreptitiously closed the lid of her laptop before he set the cup down next to it on a stack of books.

"I'm going to grab a shower, and then we can head out," Alaina said with a weak smile. She was curious, and a part of Lindsey's mind that was still alive was too.

△▽△

ADMITTEDLY, Alaina grew more and more intrigued by Noah's secrecy. Noah was nervous about something, she could tell. Alaina had healed up enough not to require as much assistance down the stairs, but Noah was still hesitating. She knew it was from nerves. He couldn't stand still, wait, or talk when he was nervous. It unsettled her. When they reached the car, the fresh air sweet and lining Alaina's nostrils, his movements were rushed and clumsy. It was only when he pulled into the street that Alaina turned to him.

"Are you okay?" she asked, concerned.

"Yes," Noah replied with a shrug, and then added, "Things have been a little weird between us lately, and I don't know how this is going to go. I guess I'm just a little nervous."

More and more of Lindsey's memories had started coming back. It was unsettling and disconcerting each time it happened. The ride was relatively quiet as they snaked their way through traffic. Alaina looked out at the passing scenery, amazed at how far civilization had come. She was used to walking everywhere and now realized that if that had still been the case, getting to town would take all day. Alaina watched as cars zipped by them, as individuals on bicycles peddled lazily on the side of the road. What unsettled her, even more, was how quickly the names of things came to her. She knew how most of them worked. She knew that she could drive a car and ride a bicycle. Things made sense to her when she didn't even know what they were.

She started recognizing the scenery from Lindsey's memories as Noah drove them to a small hill that overlooked the older buildings of the city. They weren't alone, but it was secluded enough that they could talk without being overheard. It was a little resting spot that people could use to have picnics or to stretch their legs if they were driving further.

"It's not much," he said, "but I want us to get back to the way we were."

This was the spot that they had driven past on their first date. They had decided to have their picnic here instead of at the park which they had planned. The view from their tiny hill had been stunning as the sun had set. Lindsey had loved that Noah simply went along with the sudden change. It was at this very spot that she had decided Noah was someone she wanted in her life. It was there that she'd decided that Noah would be the one she grew old with. She was going to start a family with him.

Bile rose in Alaina's throat. Lindsey barely made it past her 25th year. All of her dreams had shattered just like that. Alaina swallowed. That was not the sort of thinking she needed to be doing.

Alaina noticed the backpack he'd pulled from the car and carried with them. From within its massive interior, Noah retrieved a blanket. He laid it out carefully for them under the dappled shade of a still-growing oak tree.

"I know we usually come out here during sunset," he said with a shy smile, taking a moment to look toward the horizon where the sun would be setting in a few hours. "But, I wanted to help you remember." Noah helped Alaina into a comfortable seated position on the blanket and sat beside her. "I wanted to do something special for you, Lindsey."

Alaina held her breath at the name. Of course, it was for Lindsey. She had to keep reminding herself that Noah still thought of her as the same girl that he'd fallen in love with.

He pulled from the bag the same tattered book that he'd had with him at the hospital. Alaina recognized it from Lindsey's memories as the book she had given him on their first date. It was a cheap second-hand copy of a novel by one of his favorite fantasy authors. The book had seen better days even when Lindsey had bought it; now, it looked like it would blow apart in the wind.

Alaina smiled. "You still have that old thing?"

He nodded and passed it to her. "It reminds me of how easily things could have been different."

Alaina gently stroked the wrinkled and bent cover as she avoided eye contact with him.

"I know we've been on shaky ground lately, but I want you to know that you mean the world to me, Lindsey. And when I thought I was going to lose you…"

"I'm stronger than that. C'mon, give me some credit." Alaina laughed as Lindsey's memories filled in the gaps. Lindsey had always been a happy-go-lucky girl. The last year without her mother had changed her in ways that were affecting her and Noah's relationship. She had been moody, aggressive, and downright rude. Still, Noah hadn't gone anywhere. They'd fought, but he had never raised his voice at her and stayed even when Lindsey had tried her hardest to push him away.

Noah gave a half-hearted laugh before rummaging through the bag again.

"I brought your favorite," he said, handing her a brown paper bag. Alaina frowned at it as she carefully opened it. The smell of French fries hit her nose and made her mouth water.

"Noah," Alaina warned when she realized what was happening. Her heart started aching for a love that wasn't hers. He was desperately trying to rebuild what he'd had with Lindsey, but Alaina had no right to it. She reminded herself that she didn't want any of it, anyway. He was doing this for Lindsey. Better that he knew she wasn't coming back rather than merely dragging him along with her.

To hell with the disguise. This was not fair to Noah. Already, lives had been ruined because of her, and his life had been destroyed once before, by the accident. Was she really cruel enough to drag him along and to break his heart all over again when she died? No, Alaina wasn't a bad person. She always tried to help those in need. And right now, Noah was in need. He needed the truth.

Alaina set the bag down on the blanket and met Noah's gaze. "I…"

"Lindy, please, let's just enjoy the moment for once," His eyes showed no hint that he was going to let it go. He was dead set on enjoying this day with her. That was fine. She'd find another time to tell him what was really going on.

She snapped her mouth shut. It had been five years since their first date, and here he was trying to recreate the very thing he was so desperately yearning for. Alaina remembered her own feelings toward Damon and how he had made her feel before everything went awry.

This is ridiculous, Alaina thought. I don't have time to play this stupid, pointless game. She could feel her irritation rising, and with it, the familiar tingle of magic in her veins. Alaina's power had always been connected to her emotions. It was part of why it had taken her much longer to control her magic than her sisters or even the rest of the coven. Alaina shifted positions as if to get to her feet and opened her mouth to tell Noah to stop. It was then that her wound echoed the tingle of magic. It wasn't necessarily painful, but it was certainly an unpleasant feeling. Alaina placed her hand on her abdomen and glanced around.

Damon!

He was there, watching them. It didn't look like him, but it must have been him... There was no other explanation. She knew the tingle of his magic better than anyone.

Her heart fluttered violently in her chest, and a sour heat pooled in the pit of her stomach, her emotions warring inside of her. She wanted to reach out and touch him, and, at the same time, pin him down and tear his intestines from his body while he watched. It couldn't be him. He wasn't supposed to have the ability to track her in the first place. Especially not if her spell had worked. Had Alaina simply imagined it? Or, had she imagined feeling her magic in the first place? Alaina stared at Damon.

"Lindsey?" Her ears were ringing.

No, she decided, her power was definitely returning, still feeling the tingle of magic run through her veins as she continued to stare.

"Lindsey?" Noah had his hand on her arm and concern etched into his face, already positioned in a crouch, ready to run to the car with her. Finally, his voice penetrated her thoughts. "Lindy? Are you okay?"

"Just... it's just," Alaina took a steadying breath and smiled sheepishly. "I accidentally tugged on my stitches. I don't think I tore them open, though."

"You sure?" Noah asked, his hands hovering over her.

Alaina nodded, forcing herself to look at Noah and not at the man that was sauntering off past them. Alaina could feel his magic brush up against hers, and she desperately squashed hers down. The talons of his magic scraped its nails over hers. Teasing, testing... If he even picked up the faintest trace of her, it would be over.

He looked different, but there was no mistaking the color of his eyes. What kind of magic did he possess? Could he change his form? Was it possible to body jump?

Alaina kept her face neutral and light as the questions pounded through her head. Damon did not have that kind of magic. At least, Alaina hadn't thought so. She'd spent years training with him, and he had certainly never shown any inclination to soul and blood magic.

Damon disappeared into the crowd, and Alaina remained by Noah's side as they relived their first date. Alaina kept her composure, forcing her powers down. Noah had accepted her answer and continued talking and reading passages to her. Alaina had to suppress her anger at the fact that Noah was trying so hard. The more time she spent with him, the harder it would be to leave. And Alaina had had enough heartbreak for several lifetimes.

She needed to distract herself and found it all too easy to draw on Lindsey's memories to drive the conversation down safer paths.

"Did you get a can of that horrible orange cola?" Alaina asked, drawing on Lindsey's memory of their first date. Noah had grabbed drinks for them without checking and only realized what monstrosity he had shown up with when it was too late. Being the braver of the two, Lindsey had volunteered. Alaina could have sworn the taste of it still lingered in her mouth.

Noah grinned and pulled a single can from the back-pack. "Of course. No first date would be complete without it."

Alaina laughed and popped the can open. She stared at the fizzy liquid and inhaled the scent of sweet cola and oranges. It was strangely soothing, Alaina thought before taking a deep drink.

"Can I ask you something?" she ventured as she handed the can to Noah, suppressing a shiver at the after-taste. It lined her mouth like fish oil.

He laughed at her reaction. "Sure."

"Why did you say yes when I asked you out five years ago?"

"Oh, no, no, no. You didn't ask me, remember?" Noah laughed again. The sound was light and airy, and it lifted her spirits. "I asked you. I begged you to have pity on my poor soul and…"

"That wasn't…" Alaina felt her face burn red hot. The memory had been of him playfully begging for a kiss. One Lindsey had happily given him. A broad grin spread over Alaina's face.

"What?" Noah was confused by her cryptic smile. "What, what did I do?"

"Noah, my crazy, silly Noah." The words took her by surprise. It was instinct. Lindsey's memories took over, and she could do little to fight it. If Damon was still around, she would do well not to try.

She saw the color creep up his neck. Playing on his feelings for Lindsey was becoming almost second nature for Alaina. She drew on Lindsey's memories and copied her mannerisms, her inflection, and her thoughts.

You're a horrible person, Alaina, she chided herself.

She stuffed the thought away. I need to survive, or people like Noah will have no future to enjoy and no memories to relive. Damon and Zachariah will make sure of that.

Alaina swallowed another gulp of the horrible cola and cleared her throat. "No, I'm serious, Noah. What made you say, yes?"

He contemplated for a moment before answering, chewing on a cold fry. "I am inexplicably drawn to you, Lindy. I wanted to know you. I know we joke about it, but you really did turn my life around from the very first time we met."

Alaina was stunned. It was a revelation that, while

Lindsey was aware that he had had a rough start in life, wasn't something she had known much about. It made Alaina feel closer to him, a fact that annoyed her. She felt closer to him than Lindsey ever was.

△▽△

ALAINA DIDN'T LIKE to admit it, but she enjoyed the day with Noah. It was something that she hadn't experienced in a very long time, the carelessness of a date. It was undoubtedly much better than staring at the screen of her laptop, trying to find things about her sisters, and coming up with nothing day after day. Alaina realized she had been less than polite in her interactions with Noah.

It may have been an excellent cover to keep her off of Damon's radar, but Noah was still an innocent soul caught up in a supernatural mess. He deserved better.

Stop it!

Alaina mentally struggled with herself. There was no point in getting sentimental. Yes, Noah was taking care of her while she healed up and adjusted to this new place. Still, if she didn't find her sisters and figure out where on earth Zachariah was, there would be more significant consequences than just her feeling guilty about using him.

"What are you thinking so hard about?" Noah asked. "I can practically hear the gears grind in your head."

"I'm a little tired," Alaina said vaguely. She opened her mouth, then changed her mind and closed it, chewing on her bottom lip. Alaina inhaled sharply, and hastily said, "I actually wanted to ask you something."

"More questions? Wow, you must be feeling better."

Both Alaina and Noah chuckled, and she shook her head. "Don't be a butt." It was Lindsey's favorite non-insult, and Alaina was starting to feel as though she really was becoming comfortable in her new skin.

"All right, all right," Noah said, throwing his hands in the air.

Alaina stared at the streetlights as they leisurely drove back to the apartment, and her eye caught the flash of faraway lightning that signaled an oncoming storm. It felt a little different, both to her and when compared to Lindsey's memories. There was something in the way the lightning crackled that made the hairs on the back of her neck stand on end.

"I want to tell you something, but it's going to sound a little crazy."

Noah said nothing, but she saw his arched brow as they drove beneath a streetlight, his face briefly illuminated before falling back into shadow. He did not seem anything more than curious, so Alaina continued.

"While I was in my coma, I," Alaina began, then paused, thinking about the best way to approach this. "I saw some things."

"What things?"

"Dreams, or visions, or something. I saw things that felt very real to me."

"Okay." Noah glanced at her, and still, she saw the innocence on his face as he waited for her to continue.

"I wanted to ask if you would help me with figuring out what they were, or what they mean, and if maybe some of the things I saw were real or not." It was the only way that she might get his assistance in the matter. If she pretended that it was a dream, she might just get away with it. And she'd realized that she needed his help. He always was the techie one of the two. Lindsey didn't know Ctrl from Shift on a keyboard, and it made Alaina's life difficult.

"Is this what you've been working on?" Noah asked. Then, when he noticed the look of surprise on Alaina's face, he added, "You aren't as sneaky as you think you are."

"I don't know if that's a good or a bad thing." Alaina chuckled nervously and tucked her hair behind her ear.

"You've never been good at lying, so I'd say it's a good thing that it hasn't changed." The genuine smile of happiness on his face made her stomach turn with guilt. He was still ultimately in love with Lindsey, and it hurt. Alaina was frequently reminded of Damon's betrayal every time she saw the way Noah looked at her. It was a hard feeling to shake.

Mistaking the look on her face for something else, Noah tried to reassure her, "Hey, it's a good thing, Lindy. It means you're still you."

Alaina returned his smile, ignoring the comment. "So? Will you help?"

"Anything you need," he said.

There was a brief tingle accompanying the stab of pain at her wound as Noah slowed and stopped at a red light. He was still peppering her with questions about everything she had been up to since they'd left the hospital. Alaina briefly had the feeling they were being watched. She felt herself sitting up straighter as she scanned the darkness beyond the haloes of light.

It was faint, but she could feel the presence. Then, the light turned green, and Noah drove off. The feeling disappeared.

"Lindsey?"

"Yeah?" Alaina asked, startled.

"Where do we start?"

She glanced in the side mirror into the light-broken darkness; there was nothing. The tingle was gone, but the uneasiness remained. Alaina hesitated. She did want Noah to help. Not only because he would be a good cover in case Damon did try and probe, but it would go faster with two, and time was annoyingly short.

"Lindy? You okay?"

Again, Alaina had to suppress the tone of annoyance in her voice. "Yeah, yeah, I am." Alaina briefly explained the story about the sisters she saw and what she found.

"I want to find out what happened to them three hundred years ago. I found some information about them. They existed, they were real," Alaina said, reassuringly. It was easy to say that she saw them in a vision, but finding them was something completely different. She had to prove that they were real.

"That's a long time ago, Lindy. Are you sure we can find information on something like that?"

"I've already started looking, Noah. That's how I know it happened that long ago. I managed to find one of the sisters, but not the other." Alaina bit her lip, contemplating how much she could share without sounding even crazier than she already did.

"Wow, really?"

"Well, not find find," Alaina admitted. "I know she came to America on a ship..."

"Oh, like when people came to the New World?"

Alaina frowned as Lindsey's memories filled in the gaps. "Yeah, I guess."

Still nervous about Damon's earlier unexpected appearance, Alaina remained guarded as she asked Noah if he would help her narrow down the research.

"Of course! I've been dying to know what you've been doing, Lindy! I was driving myself nuts, thinking about all the things it could be. And now you're asking for my help, and I..."

Alaina couldn't help but smile. His energy was infectious. She didn't bother listening to what else he had to say. Instead, she kept her guard up and scanned for the energy that was following her around. With Noah's help, they might just manage to pull this thing off.

Chapter Four

Alaina's hands were shaking as she slid into the driver's seat. Sure, she had Lindsey's memories, and, in theory, it should have been enough. But remembering something in someone else's mind was a process she'd never get used to. Lindsey's memories were still patchy, and the fear of the car, the fear she had developed after a particularly gruesome dream about the accident, didn't help her much.

Still, Alaina had to do this. She had to get used to this. She couldn't rely on Noah to take her everywhere, and walking seemed more dangerous than her driving. There was only one option.

Noah, as always, was frustratingly calm and supportive as she ground the gears and stalled the car. The angrier she got, the funnier he seemed to find the entire situation.

"Want me to drive?" he asked, suppressing a smile after Alaina had glared at him.

"No," she snapped, suppressing a smile of her own. It wasn't the sort of smile she'd have if she found this funny.

No, this was a smile of frustration, a smile she knew he would have taken out of context if he'd seen it.

Alaina was aware of the harsh tone in her voice, but she couldn't quite peg the timing. When the car had stalled for the seventh time, Alaina switched it off and laid her head against the steering wheel.

"Tell me honestly," she said, sighing and looking at him with one open eye. She had a feeling that she never could drive, and Noah was just taking the opportunity to spend time with her. "Was I ever any good at driving?"

Noah exhaled a cough that, to Alaina, sounded suspiciously like a laugh. "You know how to drive if that's what you're asking."

Alaina shot him another glare. "Noah, this isn't funny. I can see what I need to do, and I remembered how, but I can't get this contraption moving."

"Deep breath, Lindy."

Alaina rolled her eyes at him, but he ignored her. She never did understand it when people told her to take deep breaths. As if that was going to help her remember how to drive a bloody car.

"You just need a little bit of practice, that's all," Noah assured her, patting her knee.

Alaina lifted her head and looked at him. He seemed to be getting used to the different personality that reared its head every once in a while, especially when Alaina was tense.

"If only teleportation had been invented," Alaina said, referring to the mode of transportation in yet another space movie Noah loved to watch.

He grinned at her. Alaina inhaled profoundly and started the car for the eighth time. After a slow start, she managed to pull out into the road and was soon a little more comfortable behind the wheel.

"Lindsey, I know I said I'd help you figure things out, but you know I need to get back to work soon."

Alaina shot him a glance and returned her eyes to the road. She was comfortable, but not so much that she would risk anything more than that.

"Are you giving up?" Alaina asked, trying not to let the hurt show.

"No, no. I'm just saying that at some point, the real world will come knocking."

It was true. Alaina knew that. She knew they were not going to be able to survive much longer if he didn't go back to work to earn a salary. They needed money, and he was the only one who could get it for them. Alaina was in no state of mind to go back to Lindsey's job at the gallery to sell those hideous, abstract paintings people in this century called art. She knew Lindsey felt the same way about those outrageous things. Besides, Alaina had much bigger things to worry about. The end of the world being one of them.

Alaina wanted to protest but stayed quiet. He wasn't aware of the magic that flowed through the world. Or the people that were able to control it. She wanted to keep him in the dark for as long as possible. It may very well be the only thing that would keep him alive. If Zachariah was making his move, the less Noah knew, the safer he would be.

"I know," she said instead, her knuckles turning white as she gripped the steering wheel. She knew she shouldn't have gotten him involved. The fact that he would soon be leaving her to her own devices. Even though she knew they had no other option. But she had gotten used to having him around, and that was her biggest mistake of all.

THE REST of the week went by in a blur. They had done some research but hadn't found a single morsel of helpful information. Still, she'd enjoyed spending time with him. She had even memorized the way his eyes lit up when he thought he found something useful. The look on his face when he realized it was another dead end was something she was trying to forget, though.

When the day came when Noah had to go back to work, he was already gone by the time Alaina rolled out of bed. She hadn't heard him come in but found the note he'd left for her next to his keys. She couldn't help but smile at the neat writing. Lindsey had endlessly mocked him for his beautiful lettering. Often asking him if he had a set of stencils stashed somewhere whenever he wrote with pen and paper. It was always said good-naturedly.

Alaina was glad her injury was healing. She could still feel the cold tickle of magic in the center of the wound, where the tip of the dagger had pierced deep into her whenever she got angry. She had practiced small spells, mostly lighting candles or helping to keep the fern in the kitchen green and happy. This made Noah suspicious. Lindsey could never keep anything alive if it didn't bark or purr. But the fern looked terrific, and it had caused a raised eyebrow from Noah the first time he'd noticed it. Alaina had merely shrugged and told him that being so close to death made her feel sorry for the plant that had suffered at her hands, or lack of them, all those months. He'd seemed to buy it and left with an eye roll and shake of his head. He had mumbled something about Lindsey being full of surprises, but she couldn't hear the rest. Still, she made sure to "forget" to water it every now and again, just to set his mind at ease.

Alaina had missed being able to do magic, even if it was just small things. She knew that as she healed and her soul eventually bound properly with Lindsey's body, she would be able to do more potent spells. The only problem was that she didn't know whether it was safe. Damon might have placed some spells on her, perhaps some to alert him when there was a significant spike in her magic. If he could body jump, he could cast any form of a spell. Alaina had to be very careful. She kept to the small spells at first, at least until such a time where she had no other option than to release the full wrath of her magic.

She boiled the kettle, still amazed that with the simple turn of a knob, she could bring fire instantly to the stove. It was a novel idea, and one of the modern world's technologies that she was most grateful for. Alaina made her tea and took her cup to the tiny balcony, where she stood by the half wall and stared out over the city.

Lindsey's memories supplied the names of the buildings, types of vehicles, and the large university where she'd worked as a teaching assistant for a year before her mother's death. They'd let her go soon after, fed up with her behavior. It wasn't glamorous, but it had allowed her to finish her post-graduate work and earn a little income at the same time.

Alaina let the girl's memories fill her, drawing inspiration from them to learn how to handle Noah. He still believed that Lindsey was alive, and Alaina needed to keep him thinking that. She needed help, whether she wanted it or not. The fact that he also acted as a shield was an added perk, but one she felt she couldn't utilize for too long.

"I have no idea how long it will take to find him," Alaina said out loud to herself. "I can't pretend to be Lindsey forever."

However accurate the statement was, Alaina found herself thinking about it a little more. Would it really be that bad if she simply walked away? She had gotten a rare second chance and defied Death himself.

To stop Zachariah.

She pursed her lips together. No matter how tempting an option, she couldn't. Not in good conscience, anyway. She couldn't walk away from something so dangerous. Zachariah could wipe out all magic and put humankind under his thumb. If he had survived the blood link...

Alaina thought again to the moment of her death, seeing each of the tiniest details with utter clarity. Things she had missed but that her mind had remembered. There was one moment in particular that stood out to her as she replayed her memories over and over again. Zachariah's panicked shout as she'd closed the magic circle drawn in her own blood on that cold, stone floor.

She drank deeply from her cup, savoring the sensation as it warmed her. Zachariah must have known what it was. Without the strength of her life force, he would not have been able to break the binding.

Alaina thought again to the way Damon had coaxed her sisters to join them. How Alaina herself had encouraged them. She had placed them in Zachariah's path.

You didn't know that she reminded herself.

"No, but I do now."

Alaina padded back inside, barefoot, feeling the carpet beneath her. It was soft and plush and clean. It wasn't just a woven rug that kept the cold from the stone floor seeping into her bones. Alaina turned the faucet and watched as water flowed smoothly into her cup. She rinsed it and set it aside, watching the water run for but a moment more, still utterly amazed at how easy things seemed to be in this new world.

Alaina returned to her desk, where her laptop was still open on the pages she had researched on the ships that had departed the New World and set sail north. The deeper Alaina tried to dig, the more frustrated she became. The records were not kept up to date, and there was little to no information on where to go next.

Alaina tapped her fingers on the keyboard, listening to the sound they made as she stroked each key. She waited for the page to load and the information to be brought to her screen. Something so small, but it still boggled her mind. Anything she had needed to note and keep track of had to be meticulously recorded on paper and stored carefully. Not only was it rare for farmers, such as they were, to know how to write, but it had also been a near miracle for women to learn. Alaina picked up a textbook and flipped through the pages. The pages weren't as thick as what she was used to, and they certainly weren't bound with the same kind of care, but perhaps in this age, they had better, faster ways to secure.

Alaina carefully placed the book back on the pile and returned to her search. She shook her head as the page yielded no new information. Alaina grunted in annoyance and pushed her seat back, staring at the ceiling and feeling the ache in her shoulders from being hunched over for an extended time.

On a whim, Alaina began a new search for strange and seemingly unnatural occurrences. She laughed as the results were returned: there were far too many.

Alaina's eyes were drawn to a blog post about strange weather phenomena that were occurring all over the city. She clicked the link and began reading. It didn't take long for the tingle in her spine to turn into a hot spark. The post had several images of the storm that had been brewing over the last few days but had yet to break. There were several comments as well as links to other pages, articles, and photographs of related unusual happenings.

Alaina followed a link in the post to a forum where people were discussing the impact and the cause of the storm. Many claimed global warming had a significant impact on the weather, which Alaina felt she needed to research more thoroughly than what little information she could glean from Lindsey's memories. While others were leaning more to the supernatural side of things.

As Alaina read message after message and went through several articles of a similar nature, she began to piece together the information. It all certainly seemed very magical in nature, but not in a way that bore Zachariah's signature. It chilled her blood. Had he somehow managed to change his own fingerprint, his own magic's personality? If he had, she was in way over her head.

ALAINA HAD FOUND information online about a couple of esoteric shops that were close to home. Noah had the car, which put a small damper on her plans, but Alaina was sure she could get around. Lindsey's memories of the city and its general layout were definitely helping Alaina get her bearings.

As Alaina locked up behind her, she felt the familiar tingle spark up again, and again she felt as though she was being watched. Alaina remained cheerful, despite feeling only marginally protected by the body she was in. She looked both ways before crossing the street and had to force herself to keep moving when she noticed Damon in the crowd. This time, there was no mistaking him.

Again, he looked different, but she knew. There was one thing that Damon could not hide from her, and that was his magical essence. Especially now that she was able to pick it up in this overwhelmingly cluttered world. She recognized it as soon as their eyes met. Alaina smiled politely and continued down the sidewalk, feigning obliviousness.

Damon may have had a suspicion about who she might really be, but she was not about to make it easy for him. Alaina changed her plans. If she was seen going into an esoteric shop, Damon would no doubt put two and two together. Surely, he must know Lindsey's patterns by now, especially if he was out looking to find changes in them. And given how little Lindsey knew about the occult and anything related to it, she was sure that the girl did not bother with those things.

Alaina detoured into a coffee shop, one of Lindsey's favorites, and got her usual order. There would be no deviating from anything today, Alaina thought miserably. The drink she received was thick, creamy, and much sweeter than Alaina had expected. Since Lindsey had her tea black and unsweetened, she had expected the same from her coffee. She'd stood and watched as they made her drink, taking in every small detail.

Alaina had not seen milk in the fridge at home, but as soon as the barista brought out the jug, it took a lot of effort not to gape. The world was so different from what she remembered. Milk had been a rare and tradable commodity. Cream, more so, and here they had gallons of the stuff on hand. All for the convenience of others.

Alaina watched, fascinated, as the barista blended ice and ice cream together before adding in the flavor syrup. When she topped it with the whipped cream and added a generous caramel drizzle, Alaina grinned from ear to ear. If anything, this had been a display of wealth. Ingredients that were hard to come by and would spoil within a day...

Alaina thanked her, leaving a tip in the jar and walking back out into the midday sun, enjoying the sweet drink.

Alaina felt giddy, excited, and happier than she had since she woke up in the hospital. She knew that Damon was still close. No doubt, he was watching her, waiting to see if she let the façade slip.

Alaina decided to delve into Lindsey's memories and follow the girl's routine. For the most part, Lindsey spent more time in the library and at the university, doing research and working than she did anywhere else.

She had hoped to visit the various magic and occult shops that were rather popular with modern humans. Unfortunately, with Damon hot on her heels, Alaina was forced to blend in and be as human as she possibly could be. And that meant she had to avoid using magic.

It made getting around a bit more complicated, but she calmly took another sip of her drink and hailed a cab.

Alaina sat idle for a while, marveling at the small changes that had happened throughout history. Curiosity had gotten the better of her, and she soon found herself surrounded by several thick tomes that told of how the world had changed. Alaina was horrified and amazed by the determination and cruelty of the human race to survive and thrive in whatever environment it found itself in.

This city was a prime example. The photos of Lindsey's hometown from hundreds of years ago looked vastly different from what she had seen outside.

Alaina had looked into the construction and original layout of the land. Trying to figure out how the city had changed and developed over time. Hoping for some clue as to where powerful ley lines would be.

If Zachariah was here, or if his agents were trying to restore him to power, there had to be a reason. If there was a power source nearby, Zachariah would undoubtedly be targeting it. Damon was still alive. No doubt kept alive by some form of Zachariah's darkest magic, and he had been at her bedside from the day she woke up. It wasn't mere coincidence.

"Saeki is missing," Alaina overheard a student whisper to her friends. Tears and sobs making her voice break and carry. Louder than she had intended, Alaina was sure.

"What happened?"

"She was supposed to meet me down at that new club last night, but she never showed. I called and texted, but she didn't reply. Her mom called me this morning and said she hadn't been home, wanting to know if she crashed at my place."

"What? How is that possible?"

The commotion of the group had caused the librarian too politely, and regrettably, ask them to quiet down, or leave. The woman was along in years, but her eyes still held life and strength. She had a sympathetic manner and offered the girl a drink of water while her friends tried to console her. While still upset by the news, people around them did not seem at all surprised.

Alaina quietly sidled up to the counter and placed the book down, looking at the group of girls with concern. "Is everything all right?" she asked, hoping to get more information.

People didn't just drop off the face of the earth, not even in a city this size. What bothered her more was the fact that people didn't really seem fazed by the news, as if this was a regular occurrence.

Lindsey's memory was triggered by the conversation. Alaina's instincts had been right. This had not been a singular event, with the disappearances happening mostly in New Orleans, which was only about an hour away. And also, only women seemed to have been targeted. A shiver ran down her spine.

Alaina offered her condolences and wandered back to her table. She made a couple of notes, returned the books to their resting places, and carefully gathered together her sheets of paper. She had gotten more information than she'd thought she would, and it would require an extra pair of eyes to go over it all.

Deciding to look into the history of New Orleans, Alaina asked the librarian a few more questions relating to those sections and topics before heading off to find them. She would use the computer to find out more about the missing women. Asking too many questions could draw unwanted attention to her, especially with Damon close by.

It was a nuisance, this man. She wished he would just leave her alone. The pain in her chest had not yet healed from his betrayal, and with him so close by, she found it hard to keep her composure.

Alaina spent hours making notes and researching landmarks. Eventually, she moved to an open computer and started researching the missing women.

Her hackles rose as she scrolled through the articles detailing the circumstances of their disappearances. They all seemed to have been chosen at random, but the tingle in the pit of Alaina's stomach warned her against that conclusion.

She found countless other pages of women, girls, children, and even men that had gone missing. Not all of them were linked to the New Orleans cases, but the impact of the darkness lurking in plain sight was clear. The mild reactions of the group made more sense to her now. Not simply because there were similar cases, but because the circumstances weren't isolated. The world she had woken up in was so different from the one she had left behind. Missing children had been a rare occurrence. The communities were smaller, more likely to notice. Out here, in a city this size...

Alaina shivered again, and an icy hand gripped her heart. The world had changed more than she'd thought. Even if Zachariah wasn't personally behind the disappearances, his magic must have had an impact on those exposed to it over the years. If not his magic, then, Alaina thought, it must have been the inherent darkness within the human race.

His agents could be out there, right now, looking for more victims. With a sudden realization, her wound flared painfully, and her skin prickled as her magic surged. Zachariah was alive, and he was looking to regain his power.

Alaina quickly shut down the computer and gathered her notes, leaving the books where they were. The confines of the library suddenly made her relive the moment of her death. She struggled to draw breath, and her vision swam.

She'd hoped that Zachariah hadn't survived.

Stupid, stupid.

Alaina clutched her notes as, on the smooth pages, she subconsciously traced the very same symbols that she had traced as she lay dying. Alaina would need more potent magic. She needed her sisters. The bond between her and Zachariah would not have broken if they were resurrected in their new bodies. As long as their souls existed, so did the bond.

Was that why she was resurrected here? In this century? Was she resurrected here because Zachariah was, too, or because this was where he wanted her? She could only hope he didn't know about the bond.

Alaina needed Brenna and Morgan. She didn't have the power to stop him alone. She hadn't had it three hundred years ago, and she certainly did not have it now.

Chapter Five

ALAINA RETURNED HOME, EXHAUSTED FROM SUPPRESSING her own magic. She could feel it like a physical force pressing down on her, tiring her muscles. She felt like a balloon that was pumped too fully with air, as though she might burst at any moment. Alaina had never realized how hard it was to keep her magic suppressed. It was a hard feat, one she wasn't sure how long she would be able to keep up. Not when there was so much to do and so little time.

There was a ripple, as a breath shuddered out of her. She felt her magic expand from its confines. Alaina closed her eyes, running through the information in her head. She'd gone to the public records office as soon as she had left the library. Something she'd had to ask directions for from an ornery old man, to find more information on the ship that had come in from South America.

Zachariah was rising. Or, perhaps, he had already risen. Without using her magic, Alaina couldn't be sure. And with Damon haunting her every step, she couldn't risk it. More than ever, she needed to find her sisters. Morgan was in the wind. Maybe hiding, maybe dead, but she doubted it. She was here somewhere; Alaina could feel it. If only she would show herself. If only Alaina could send out a wave of her magic, alerting her sister of her existence, of her presence. But she couldn't, and it frustrated her. She couldn't send out any kind of signal without alerting Damon, or worse, Zachariah. Her mind was exhausted, and she found herself drifting off on the couch, curled into a tight ball. Her dreams were haunted by Damon's face.

When she woke, Alaina was covered in a sheen of sweat, and her wound was throbbing painfully. She shivered, disoriented in the dark, and heard the keys jangle in the lock. Without really thinking, Alaina launched herself off the couch, ignoring the painful tugging beneath her bandages. She grabbed the closest thing she could find, a lamp, and pulled it out of the wall. A clatter of objects fell from the table next to the couch as she knocked them over, but she didn't care. She stepped closer, holding the lamp like she would a baseball bat, ready to swing.

"Lindy?" Noah called.

Alaina could hear him shuffling around in the kitchen as he dropped the keys into the bowl and hung his jacket on the coat rack.

Her heart was still hammering in her chest when Noah stepped through the archway that led to the living room. His eyes lingered on the lamp. "Lindy, what the hell?"

Alaina exhaled sharply and closed her eyes, dropping the lamp to her side. "I thought you were an intruder." Not the whole truth, but not a lie either.

"You were going to beat them up with a lamp?"

Alaina could see the smirk on his features as his eyes twinkled mischievously. She huffed, "Don't be a butt!"

Noah pressed his lips together and smiled at her,

reaching for the lamp. "I'm sorry for being a little late, Lindy. I was just catching up on some of the paperwork that I got behind on. They had a temp fill in for me while I was in the hospital, but she never showed up today. Then, management and I had a meeting regarding upcoming changes."

"Do you need to go back on Monday?" Alaina asked, her hope slowly diminishing as she realized that Noah may have no choice but to choose work over helping her. It was a good job, and he made enough for them to live reasonably comfortably. Alaina knew from Lindsey's memory that Noah had worked hard to get as far as he did, given the rough start he'd had.

"No." He shook his head, setting the lamp down on the counter. He examined the damage. "I still have a few days of medical leave left."

Alaina sighed with relief. "What did they want to discuss?"

"They want to assign me, my own technical team."

"That's awesome, Noah!" Alaina was genuinely excited at the news. It wasn't just a remnant of Lindsey floating around in her head. She had learned a lot about Noah and Lindsey by studying her memories, and in her own way, she was starting to care for him.

"But," he continued his sentence as if she hadn't interrupted him, "I told Sean I'd need to think about it."

"What? Why would you do that? Isn't this what you wanted?"

"Lindy," Noah said, gently taking her hand in his, "I want to be here for you, to help you sort through this. Taking on a new position right now won't allow me to do that."

Alaina swallowed as tears threatened to blur her vision and cleared her throat. "I know I asked for your help, but you should take the offer, Noah. It's what you've been working up to for a long time."

Noah gave her his warmest smile. "Let me do this with you, Lindy."

△▽△

"I THINK Brenna is buried here, in Louisiana. I went to the library today and then down to the public records office."

"Really?" Noah asked, clearly surprised at the amount of energy she had spent researching some obscure thing. She realized how crazy she must have sounded.

She was reading so much into a "dream," something she didn't even know was real. At least, as far as he knew. But she couldn't tell him anything about what was really going on. Even if she could, she couldn't risk losing his help. She needed him, and if she had to lie to him to get him to help, so be it.

Alaina ignored the look on his face and continued, "I found some information that could lead to her grave. It doesn't say where she is, but the records did indicate that other passengers came in on the same ships and moved away from the port cities looking for other work."

"Louisiana is a big place, Lindsey," Noah said, rubbing the back of his neck. "What do you suggest we do? Go from cemetery to cemetery and look at gravestones, hoping to find hers. Going on the assumption that she even had one?"

Alaina bit back a retort.

"I'm not saying no, Lindy. We just need a better plan."

Alaina agreed. While she was in a rush to find her sister, she knew Noah was right. There would be no use in wasting time running around searching for a smaller needle in a stack of needles. Alaina bit her lip in contemplation.

"Tell me what you found out, maybe we can narrow the search," Noah offered.

Alaina grabbed her notes and swept books off the coffee table. They made hollow thumps as they hit the carpet and landed at odd angles, bending some of the pages. She laid out the notes she had taken from the library, her whole body vibrating from tension.

Noah said nothing as he watched her. Alaina was sure that he was becoming increasingly concerned with her changing behavior. Still, she could only worry about finding Brenna. Noah loved Lindsey. But she was no longer around, and as much as Alaina tried to deny it, it hurt to know that Noah did not see her when he looked at her.

He knelt beside her and listened as she explained her notes and research to him.

"I also found this," Alaina said, sliding a copy of an old photograph to him. "It's the ship that was supposed to lay anchor in Virginia."

"But it didn't make it?" Noah didn't bother looking at the photograph, only studied her face.

"It was driven off course by a storm, and they decided to dock in Louisiana."

Noah looked at Alaina, and she could have sworn that he could see into her soul. "This is great, Lindy!"

"I think we should start in the port city of New Orleans," Alaina said firmly. "It's the closest we've come to an answer."

"Did you find any other information?"

"Nothing," she admitted with a huff. "Nothing but what I have here. The Internet, for all its wonders, is surprisingly void of documentation."

Noah laughed. "The documents are old, Lindsey. They

probably kept records where the ship docked. They would have had to, especially if there were foreigners on that ship."

The two of them worked through the information together. Noah had her laptop open next to him and fed in detail as they went, organizing the data and eliminating other potential port cities.

"What is this?" Noah asked as he slid out a stray sheet from beneath a photocopied section of a map.

Alaina recognized it as the notes she'd made regarding the missing women. On the back was a crudely drawn map of suspected ley lines overlapping the existing city.

"I remembered seeing a poster of a missing girl, and then someone else was taken yesterday." Alaina didn't know how to tell him any of this. She had to think very, very carefully about what she was going to say.

Noah stared blankly at her.

"I heard some people talking in the library today." Alaina licked her lips and tucked a stray lock of hair behind her ear. "They explained the situation."

"You think there's a connection between the girls and the dreams?" Noah was quick.

Alaina shrugged. "I'm actually not sure, but it kinda stuck with me, so I did look into it a little bit."

Noah pointed to the map. "What about these dots and squiggles? And what are," Noah squinted to read her handwriting, "ley lines?"

Alaina flushed guiltily.

Noah hadn't seen her reaction but was staring at the map. "It looks like the dots are mostly concentrated around this one park." He pulled up a map of New Orleans and zoomed in, comparing the images.

"Some kind of energy source?" he murmured to himself as he dragged the map around to get a better look.

Noah was really quick.

Alaina had a gnawing feeling that she had to be even more careful about what she told him in the future. He was too quick and understood too much. She had to stay one step ahead of him, but she didn't know how to since neither she nor Lindsey had the brainpower to do so. Perhaps not even if she combined the two.

Noah was too smart for his own good.

△▽△

"WHAT WAS IT LIKE?" Noah asked later that night after dinner.

"What was what like?" Alaina asked as she dried the dishes and packed them away.

"Your coma. What was it like in there? You keep telling me that you saw things, but you've never really explained," Noah said, chewing on his thumbnail, a nervous habit he had picked up over the years. And one that had annoyed Lindsey. Alaina, on the other hand, had found the habit endearing and smiled to herself whenever she caught him doing it.

"It was…" Alaina paused, trying to find the right words. She didn't want to weird him out any more than she had already. "It was like a dream. A very vivid dream."

"I want to know what it was like for you. Please tell me?"

Alaina carefully hung the dishrag over the drying rack as she readied her thoughts. She had expected him to ask, but not quite so soon. The memory of Damon's betrayal still stung her deeply, and it was one memory she was hoping to bury.

Alaina took Noah by the hand as Lindsey had done thousands of times in the past and led him to the couch.

The light from the television was flickering mutely as they got comfortable.

"It was a very different time, Noah. There weren't cars or massive buildings. Life was simpler." Alaina smiled, surprised by the hungry look in his eyes as he listened intently while she started her story. Alaina had decided to tell him the truth under the guise of it being 'just a dream.'

"Simpler?"

She smiled, "Okay, so not really simpler, but it wasn't as confusing for me as it was when I woke up in that hospital room. Everything felt so real to me. My two sisters, my brother, and I worked in the fields alongside my mother and father."

"I find that hard to imagine," Noah said playfully.

Alaina gently smacked his arm. "Don't be a butt, Noah. I'm busy telling a story."

Noah made a zipper motion with his fingers over his lips. He kept quiet, his eyes twinkling mischievously in the light of the television.

"We worked hard, and we kept the family secret." Alaina paused and saw the curiosity flare in his eyes. She chuckled, leaning in closer and lowering her voice. "We were the most powerful family in town. We could all do magic." She sat back and shrugged. "To one degree or the other, anyway."

His eyebrows shot up, but he said nothing.

"We used our powers to keep the crops healthy and the yields high, even during the harshest of droughts." Alaina could still smell those fields. She missed it so very much.

"Weren't you scared of getting caught?"

"Not at first," she admitted. "It wasn't quite like the Salem stories we heard growing up."

Noah waited, allowing Alaina to gather her thoughts. It may have been a harder time, but she had felt freer then.

She could still feel the sun beating down on her as she coaxed a tiny seedling to grow stronger. Magic hadn't been controlled back then.

"What happened when you woke up?" Noah turned to her so he could watch her without twisting his neck to the side. "What made you decide to dig so deeply into these dreams?"

"It was the day I died."

Noah frowned, and Alaina could see the connection he was trying to make in his mind. The doctor had told her that it had gotten dicey on the operating table. It had been touch and go for a while.

"I was betrayed by..." Alaina stopped herself before she could say 'boyfriend.' She didn't want to give Noah the wrong idea. "By a friend. His master wanted our powers for himself, and he started with me."

"What about your sisters and brother?"

Alaina cringed, deciding that it was best only to mention her sisters. "They were smart in not trusting him. I was young when I first met him and trusted him fully, too eager, and thirsty for knowledge to care. To me, he was this great warlock who taught me more powerful magic during a time when my family refused to do more than the bare minimum to keep the farm thriving. I think they knew something big was coming, but I didn't care."

"You said you were a powerful family? Why weren't they there for you?"

Alaina swallowed hard, her body already beginning to shake as she recalled the moment the blade went in. "They didn't know who his master was or what they were planning. Not until it was too late."

Noah took her hand in his and stroked the back of her knuckles as she shivered.

"My sisters came around eventually, also eager to learn

new magic and new spells, but after Brenna had an argument with Damon, they both left. They broke off from us to form their own coven." Alaina had a rueful smile on her face and a faraway look in her eyes. "They saw him for who he really was long before I blindly followed him into that building." Alaina shook her head. "I had roped in a few girls from my sister's coven. I thought I was so smart at the time. Unfortunately, they died that day, too. I still feel the blade inside of me. I can still see those... dreams when I close my eyes."

Alaina desperately held on to the small amount of hope that was blooming in her chest. She wasn't quite sure exactly what she was hoping for, but she wanted him to believe her.

"Wow, Lindy. That..." Noah trailed off and then remained quiet for a while, digesting. Again, Alaina flinched at the name. It wasn't her name that he had used, but the name of the girl he loved. She closed her eyes and forced her emotions under control.

Alaina cleared her throat, "What else do you want to know?"

"What are you hoping to find, researching all of this?" Noah indicated the growing stack of books that had organically started to grow on the coffee table.

"Zachariah, the man that took my powers, will destroy the world as we know it. I believe that these dreams were leading me to find and stop his magic from spreading. I felt and saw first-hand what he was capable of."

"Lindy, do you hear yourself?" Noah was suddenly angry. Alaina blinked in bewilderment as he continued. "All this talk of magic. It's one thing to think of this as a dream, but you're making it sound like you've been sent on this... this ridiculous quest."

"I can't explain it, Noah. All I know is that I need to

stop this. I have to." Alaina could feel tears welling up and refused to let them fall. The stress of the last week had taken its toll. She was angry and frustrated, and most of all, she desperately wanted him to believe her. She was tired of pretending.

"I need to find and stop this evil from rising again. If I don't find them, and if I don't stop this, this monster will keep doing what he's doing. Those girls that went missing were probably used in dark and bloody rituals." Her words hit harder than they should have. For the first time, she let herself imagine the horrors that those girls were going through.

"Lindsey, it was three hundred years ago." Noah shook his head. "Even if it was true somehow and you got this vision thing from this girl, no man can live that long."

Alaina blinked as her vision swam. She felt her lip quiver but clenched her jaw. She was not going to cry.

"Lindy," Noah said and wrapped a gentle arm around her shoulders, "I love you, and as crazy as it sounds to me, I know that maybe this is something that you just have to do."

"Like when you bought that motorcycle and wrecked it three days later?" Alaina offered, chuckling at the memory. Lindsey had warned him against buying the deathtrap. Still, in true rebellious fashion, he had gone ahead and purchased the bike only to end up in the emergency room, his leg in a cast.

Noah grimaced. "You remember that, but you still forgot that you drink honey in your tea."

Alaina blushed. Back in her own time, Alaina hadn't even contemplated drinking honey in her tea. She didn't have the sweet tooth that Lindsey had. At first, the honey had tasted odd, leaving a weird aftertaste. Still, after a whole cup, then another, Alaina had started to see the appeal. Still, the face she'd made the first time she had tasted the honey was something Noah would never let go of.

"I will help you, okay?" Noah said, lifting her chin. "I want to help, but promise me…"

"Noah."

"Promise me," Noah stressed the word, "that we will come home and start building our lives again. We can't keep running from the real world."

Alaina nodded. "I promise."

It was harder than she'd thought to make the promise. She was sure that once she had found her sisters, things would be different. Not just for her, but for Noah too. It may well be a promise that she wouldn't be able to keep. Lindsey was dead, and without Alaina, there was no soul to pilot the body.

If it was the real world that Noah was after, he would be in for the biggest shock of his life.

△▽△

"LINDY?" Noah asked quietly.

Alaina had let Noah use the bed while she continued working on their plan. She'd contacted several Wiccan covens to see if they knew anything about Brenna. She had even reached out to the more traditional witch covens. Some had turned into dead ends, mostly members masquerading as actual witches. Nothing more than empty hopes and inflated heads.

"Yeah?" The room was dark, so Alaina could not make out any detail on his face, but she could tell by his silhouette that he was looking at her.

"Do you remember the accident?"

"I…" Alaina paused. It was a touchy subject for him,

and she knew that she'd been avoiding it since they'd left the hospital. "Yeah."

"What do you remember?" She could hear the caution in his voice as if he were handling a venomous snake that could strike at any moment.

"I remember most of it, Noah. I remember that we were going to get takeout."

"We were going to get pizza," Noah confirmed. She could hear the faint smile in his voice, marred by the recollection of that day.

"We were fighting about something," Alaina stated. "We seemed to have been fighting a lot more than usual."

Noah grunted in agreement.

"I don't even remember what we were fighting about. I just remember being so incredibly angry with you."

"We were fighting about everything, Lindy. Anything, really. I was stressed and retaliated with anger because I didn't know how to deal." Noah stopped short.

"Deal with me, you mean?" Alaina took a steadying breath. Lindsey's memory had allowed her to feel the anger she'd felt during that particular fight. It had felt similar to how Alaina herself felt about Damon. Lindsey had been in a bad place and had lashed out at everyone. Noah being the closest, most natural target.

"I went out of my way to hurt you, Noah," Alaina said, drawing on Lindsey's memories again. "I started screaming at you, knowing it would get a rise out of you."

"It worked," Noah admitted.

"I remember you looked at me then, and away from the road. It was just for a minute, but it was long enough."

"I'm sorry, Lindy. I don't know how to explain to you what it felt like, waking up outside of the car surrounded by flashing lights and sirens, and not being able to get to you."

"I..." Alaina carefully thought over her words. "I don't blame you for the accident, Noah."

"I need your forgiveness, Lindy. It doesn't matter that you don't blame me. It matters that I blame myself."

Alaina went to the bed and sat down next to him. She could feel his body heat against her skin. It was strangely comforting.

"I forgive you, Noah," she said quietly, pressing her forehead to Noah's in the same way that Lindsey would have.

Noah wrapped his arms around her and pulled her down, holding her to him. She felt his body shake, and more guilt flooded her. "Thank you, Lindy," Noah laughed happily, still holding on to her, burying his nose in the nape of her neck.

"You need some rest, Noah. We'll be leaving soon," Alaina said and started pulling away.

"Stay? Please?"

Alaina's stomach turned uneasily. Those two words burned through her, knowing that it came from vulnerability made it harder for her to turn him down.

"I'm not expecting anything from you, you know that, right? I just need to feel you next to me."

The unadulterated need in his voice decided for her. Alaina scooted onto the bed and allowed him to wrap his arms around her. She lay awake for a long while, listening to Noah's breathing as he slept peacefully. Thoughts of Damon came unbidden, and Alaina cried into her pillow. For the first time since she'd woken up in the hospital, Alaina allowed her emotions to flow freely as tears and sobs were absorbed by the soft barrier and the quiet darkness in the room.

Chapter Six

THE DRIVE THROUGH TO NEW ORLEANS TOOK LESS TIME than Alaina had initially calculated. After Noah pointed out the convergence of the ley lines, Alaina had decided that this would be the most likely place to start their search. If anything, at least they would be gathering more information that would point them in the right direction.

And direction was what she needed more than anything.

"Just look at this place," Noah commented, staring at the buildings as they slowly drove past. He had the same innocent look of a child as he took in the scenery.

Alaina smiled and referenced the map on his phone as it gave directions. It was yet another remarkable technology about the world she was in. It made traveling a lot less stressful. Alaina had felt perfectly content without her smart device. Lindsey's phone had been damaged beyond repair during the accident, and Alaina hadn't really given it much thought. She had relied on messengers three hundred years ago or had delivered news and information herself. Now she had no one except Noah to talk to anyway.

Alaina had briefly considered dipping into Lindsey's savings to get a new phone but ultimately decided against it. Although Alaina felt it would be more convenient to have the device, she rarely thought of using it. Alaina remembered everything she needed, and what was too important to forget was written down and carried in a small backpack she had brought along for the trip. Besides, it felt wrong to use a dead woman's money while Alaina pretended to be her. She thought it better to survive on the bare minimum than to splurge on something as useless to her as a phone.

They pulled into the hotel parking lot and sat in the car for a few seconds before disembarking. Alaina was nervous. She hadn't seen Damon yet, but she was sure he would be keeping track of her. She didn't know how she was going to keep him at bay without exposing her secret to Noah.

"Why don't I get us settled in, and you head to the public records office?" Noah offered as he grabbed their bags from the backseat.

"You sure?" Alaina asked, stuffing more notes and loose sheets into a folder.

"Yeah, take the car, Lindy. I'll hoof it. The park isn't that far from here. We can meet back at the hotel in a few hours, grab lunch, and take it from there."

This was good. This was great. With Noah out of the way, there was a bigger chance that she could face Damon without having to expose herself. Alaina prayed to any god that would listen that Damon didn't confront her in any way, though.

On second thought, maybe it would be better to stick together.

"No, I mean, don't you want to stay together?" Alaina asked.

"We've got the whole weekend, Lindy." Noah grinned happily at her. "As they say, divide and conquer."

Alaina laughed and grabbed the keys from him. "Divide and conquer."

△▽△

ALAINA FLIPPED THROUGH THE PAGES, then back again, scanning each carefully. She was sure there were missing papers and registration documents. She shook her head and sighed just as a clerk wandered past her.

"Excuse me?" she called.

"Yes, miss? How can I help?" The clerk was a mousy woman with small, brown eyes and spectacles that seemed far too small for her head. She was skeletal, and her bony fingers gave Alaina the chills.

"Is this everything from this docket number?" Alaina asked, handing the clerk the scribbled number on a piece of paper.

"I think so," the clerk said, contemplating the answer. "But, let me double-check for you."

"Thank you," Alaina said. She turned back to the records, losing herself in them. There were definitely some things missing. There were gaps. They weren't even subtle about it. Either the documents had been tampered with, or there had been a grave mistake in the filing. If the former was the case, she knew she was on the right track.

"Miss?"

Alaina turned in her chair. "Yes?" It was a different clerk, one who was much older than the young lady who had been assisting her. Her steel gray hair was pulled into a tight bun, and she peered over her small glasses at Alaina as she approached. Did everyone wear these ridiculously small glasses? Was it part of their uniform?

She had the scrap of paper between her fingers. She seemed to be particularly interested in the documents herself, glancing at the page that lay open in front of Alaina.

The woman stretched out her hand, the sleeve of her shirt exposing her wrist. Alaina could make out a small intricate design before the woman pulled her sleeve down to cover it again. "These are all the available documents related to that case."

"Everything?" Alaina asked with disappointment.

"Yes, miss," the graying clerk said. She didn't leave immediately, and Alaina pressed her again.

"I'm looking for family," she explained.

The woman's perfectly drawn eyebrow arched high into her hairline.

"Distant family," Alaina added. "She was supposed to be on this ship." Alaina pointed at the photograph, and as she did, she noticed a small, intricate symbol stamped in the corner of the picture.

"What is this?" she asked, leaning down to get a closer look. It was a little faded, but there nonetheless. It was hard to miss.

"I'm sorry, Miss, I couldn't say."

"You must know," Alaina insisted. "Surely, you know what this symbol means? It looks like a signature of some sort."

"I'm sorry, Miss, I really couldn't say. This is all the documentation we have access to." She didn't seem at all irritated with Alaina, which made Alaina more uncomfortable that she should have been. Lindsey's memories told her that any form of a clerk did not like having to repeat themselves.

Alaina watched as the woman held her hands up in a placating gesture, her tattoo peeking out again. Alaina opened her mouth to protest but nodded in defeat. Her eyes lingered on the symbol for a few seconds before Alaina returned to the files.

The woman wasn't going to be of any help, Alaina decided, and she started flipping through the pages, finding more and more of those little symbols. Alaina suspected that they represented a sort of calling card. The missing documentation had been removed and stored elsewhere by whoever the symbol belonged to.

This was far too suspicious to be a coincidence. Brenna was here, Alaina knew it. If the missing documentation wasn't enough to go on, the magic in the air was. She could feel it, vibrating in her bones. Brenna... She was here. The magic was intense, as if a coven was nearby. Alaina could feel the different magics, but one stood out. It felt ancient and powerful. It was no longer alive but still lingered.

Someone wanted to hide Brenna. There was no other reason to keep those records hidden, other than to keep secrets. Someone knew who Brenna was and had gone to great lengths to make her disappear.

Alaina looked around her; the record room was empty again except for her. The woman had walked off. Alaina withdrew a slightly crumpled sheet of paper from inside her backpack and traced the symbol. It wasn't of any magic she knew, but she recognized some of the smaller, inner patterns as part of a binding spell. The symbol itself would hold no power, but it was interesting to her that there was at least some accuracy in the drawing. Alaina was sure it was used instead as an identifier, sort of like a secret handshake for select groups of individuals.

There had to be a way to contact them. If they knew

who Brenna was, they would also know where the documents were. More importantly, they might know where Brenna was.

Alaina returned the documentation and files to their respective boxes, setting them neatly on the table before she went in search of the woman. There was a security person stationed outside of the room that prompted her to open her bag. After a thorough search, the man radioed a clerk, and they waited in silence.

The elderly clerk double-checked the boxes, and, after ensuring that everything was still present, allowed Alaina to leave. Alaina could feel the woman's eyes on her as she left the building. A familiar tingle told her that there was more to her than met the eye.

△▽△

ALAINA WAS SEATED on a bench outside of the records office. She didn't know where to go from there, not with this quest, anyway. There were so many missing pieces, so many things that didn't make sense. And the symbol. What the hell was that symbol? Alaina sighed with frustration. Everything led to a dead-end, and there was nothing she could do about it.

Even with Lindsey's knowledge of this world etched in her mind, she didn't know enough to really help Alaina in any way. Lindsey lived in a shell and didn't like coming out of it around anyone, but Noah. She was set in doing things one way, to hell with any other way. As efficient as this might have been for Lindsey, it meant she lacked a lot of basic knowledge about the world. Alaina had tried the basics that Lindsey knew. Beyond that, she didn't know where to go or what to do.

Alaina suddenly felt a presence next to her. Felt was the

right word, she knew. She could feel the radiating magic, she could smell the thyme. Alaina turned her head to find the old clerk sitting next to her. There was a different look to her now. Her glasses were in her hands, and her friendly face was pulled into a tight purse. She seemed serious as if something was weighing on her chest.

"You said that you were looking into those records to find family. You are not the first person to come around snooping through them and telling me that story." The woman didn't look at Alaina as she spoke.

"I didn't lie when I said that I had family on that ship," Alaina reassured the woman, feeling the need to defend herself.

The woman nodded. "You are the first person that I believe. I could smell the truth on your breath when you told me. However, I did sense something else, too. You are not who you say you are, are you?"

This woman was a witch. That was the pulsing magic she had felt in the office. This woman was powerful. Alaina swallowed. But if she was working with Damon, No, if she was working with Damon, Alaina would already be dead. He wouldn't play with his food again. Not after what she did last time. If she died, so did Zachariah. Damon was bound to know that it was her.

"What makes you say that?" Alaina asked.

She knew the answer. There was a truth to magic. There was no disguising it. It was raw and told a million stories at once. There was more identity in a witch's magic than there was in their face. If this woman really was a witch, she could tell. Alaina wasn't familiar enough with the magic in the air to determine which belonged to whom. But as a local, probably knowing the scent of every witch and warlock's magic, a stranger's magic was like a neon sign.

Alaina had warded herself against people who wanted to harm her. If this woman could sense her magic, Alaina knew that she might have gotten an ally.

"Your magic and your face don't match," was all she said before lighting a cigarette. She stared at the building in front of them. It was a quaint little florist's shop. The lilies in the windows were breathtaking.

"What if I told you I came from a different time?" Alaina teased the woman with information, and the woman smiled.

"Then, I would tell you that we have waited a long time for you, Alaina, blood of Brenna."

Alaina smiled. "You know who I am?"

"Your magic feels wrong for this era. It doesn't have the watered-down taste we get nowadays. It feels like the magic Brenna left behind." The woman took a drag of her cigarette before turning to Alaina.

Alaina bit her lip and tucked a curl behind her ear; something of Lindsey's that Alaina might never shake off. Alaina's heart pounded in her throat. She didn't think it had sunken in yet. She'd found more witches, a whole coven, maybe. And Brenna. Brenna was here.

"So, Brenna came through here, then?"

The woman nodded. "Yes, but that is all I can tell you."

"Why?"

"Because the coven requires you to pass a test. Despite the taste of your magic, you could still be someone that wishes our coven harm. If you can pass the test, you will be entitled to the information you seek." Another drag, then a puff of smoke.

"Let's get to it, then." Alaina looked at the sky, determining that it was well past 11 am. Noah would get worried soon, but she had to do this first.

The woman led Alaina back into the records office, down to the basement and into an empty room with nothing but the two witches inside. Alaina could feel the energy oozing from the walls. They were trapped. This room was warded, and any magic that left their bodies in that room would never see the light of day.

The clerk started chanting. It was a chant that Alaina knew well. It was a chant that Alaina herself had created.

"Resurgemus nos a terra. Non revertetur ad terram. fratribus et sororibus sumus, non tenetur per potentiam et sanguine." The woman's Latin was flawless, and Alaina smiled to herself as she recited the familiar oath. Alaina, Brenna, and Morgan had sat in their room one evening, creating this very oath. They had just formed their coven and needed something to represent their bond and power.

"Qui traderet nos in manu nostra cadet. Cum magica, et luna, terra, et vincere eos qui resistunt veritati nobis," Alaina finished the oath. She knew it by heart. It was etched inside of her for all eternity. She had recited it enough to make sure of that.

"I am afraid that is wrong, miss," the woman said, rolling her shoulders. "I must ask you to leave."

"What?" Alaina raised an eyebrow. "I wrote that oath by hand. Do tell me what your correct version of the ending is."

"Qui traderet nos in manu nostra cadet. Cum magica, terram, et solem, et vincere eos qui resistunt veritati nobis."

Alaina laughed. "The sun? With magic, earth, and sun? The right answer is the moon."

The woman grinned. "That is correct." Then, something unexpected happened. The woman embraced her. It was the sort of hug one would only accurately describe as a bear hug. Alaina chuckled at the woman's reaction and returned the gesture.

"You have no idea how long I have waited for you, Alaina," the woman said, emotion lacing her words. "We give the test to anyone who claims to be a descendant of the Great Sisters. Anyone who doesn't argue the legitimacy of the oath gets kicked to the curb. That is if they can even recite it."

"Who are you?" Alaina's question hung in the air.

"I am Dorothy. You may call me Dot. I am the descendant of Brenna."

△▽△

ALAINA SAT in the car in front of the motel for a good couple of minutes. She had blown Noah off to meet with Dot's coven. Her coven. The coven Brenna had created and left for Alaina when she finally came back.

They had been waiting for her, all of them.

She was in their legends, the mighty and brave witch, who, during the betrayal of her beloved, still managed to take down the greatest evil of all. The coven had pledged their loyalty to her, and even though she was ecstatic about it, she had no one to share it with. She was finally getting somewhere with the quest, but she couldn't tell Noah. How could she? "A coven of witches recognized me as their 300-year-old leader?" It was crazy. She had to think of a way to tell him where she was, what she was doing, and how she'd found out that Brenna was, in fact, here.

And the symbols, the symbols she saw in the records all led to the coven that her sister created. Dot told her about a tattoo parlor about twenty minutes from Noah and Lindsey's apartment, a salon for the supernatural. They lived by the same rules the coven did and waited for Alaina in the same way.

What were they expecting from her? She was only one

person. She was one person who didn't have 300 years' worth of magical experience. She was still just a girl who had been in limbo for centuries. Her nerves were in pieces, and she didn't know what to do. She didn't know how she was ever going to do what they were expecting of her. How was she going to take down Zachariah again?

Through the coven, she had learned that Morgan was indeed alive, but no one had seen her in centuries. She was in hiding, and there was no indication that she was going to show herself anytime soon. Alaina needed to find her, and she needed the witches' help to do that. Alaina had involved Noah in this, and now she wished she hadn't. He was under the impression that they had to do this together, but with the new information and no way to tell him how she got it, it was clear that she had to put an end to their adventure. It didn't matter how much it pained her to do so.

Finally, working up the courage to go to their room, Alaina made her way from the car to the building. The hall looked much shorter than it had when they'd arrived, and before she knew it, she was in front of their door. Alaina didn't have to know what number they were in. She could feel Noah's energy on the other side of the door. With the coven now bound to her, she had more power than she had in weeks. She'd forgotten what it felt like to be this power-ful. It was refreshing. It was addictive.

Alaina entered the room without knocking.

She found him with his hands in his hair, sitting on the end of the double bed. When he looked up, his eyes told her everything that she already knew was going through his mind. Where was she? How could she do this? Was she alive? What if something happened to her? Did she crash the car? Did she finally leave me? Alaina's heart ached. This was not going to be a pleasant exchange of words.

"Lindy," he breathed, getting up from his seat and walking toward her faster than she could register. He hugged her, and his scent soothed her, sandalwood and leather. "Where have you been? I was worried sick."

"I'm sorry," she said when he finally let her go. "I got caught up with something."

Anger flared in his eyes, but instead of his usual silence, his voice boomed through the room. "You got caught up with something? Lindsey, don't you realize how worried I was? You've been acting crazy since you woke up, and then you just vanish for hours? What the hell? What the hell is going on with you?"

"I…" Alaina started, but was silenced with a raised hand.

Noah shook his head. "Something is up with you, and as much as I have tried, I cannot seem to get to the bottom of it."

"I know all this," Alaina said, tucking a lock of hair behind her ear. "But I found some things and… and I'm sorry. I didn't have a phone to contact you."

Noah sighed, defeated. He knew that he was not going to get through to Lindsey. Lindsey, who was no longer his Lindsey. All he could do was support her. Knowing this made Alaina feel increasingly guilty. She didn't want to use him anymore. But Dot had made her realize even more that she needed him. Damon and Zachariah were still out there, and they were still looking for her. Noah's presence made it less likely for them to attack her. They wouldn't risk it if they weren't 100% sure that she was indeed Alaina. Noah also knew a lot more about this world than Lindsey did, and Alaina needed everything she could get. "What did you find?"

"Brenna was here. She's buried in the cemetery just outside of town."

Noah raised an eyebrow. "All of this was in the records?"

Alaina gnawed on her lip before shaking her head. "The clerk that helped me is Brenna's descendant. I was with her all day. She told me about Brenna. What she did here, the family she had."

"So, now what?"

Alaina sighed. "Brenna's not going to be of any use to me. I need to find where Morgan ended up. We need to get some clues here. Maybe Morgan and Brenna kept in contact. I don't know."

Noah rubbed the back of his neck, obviously second-guessing her sanity. He nodded regardless. "If there are clues here, we will find them. Just promise me this," he said, grabbing Alaina's full attention. She nodded for him to go on. "Never disappear like that again."

Chapter Seven

ALAINA AND NOAH FOUND THEMSELVES HITTING DEAD END after dead end in New Orleans. There was no way that they were going to find Morgan with the information they'd managed to gather. There was only one thing left to do, and that was to use the coven to track Morgan down. It was risky, and it was going to put Alaina on Damon's radar, but what other choice did she have? She had to find Morgan to take down Zachariah. Alaina couldn't do it by herself, that much she knew. Zachariah was much too strong. Even with her new coven, there was nothing she could do alone to stop him.

Alaina looked at the group of witches in the living room. As promised, they'd come to her aid as soon as she'd asked for it. In the week since their trip, Alaina had gotten herself a phone and called Dot to arrange the meeting. They had to come to her apartment, and although it was an hour-long trip, every single one of the witches had arrived.

There were eight of them. The coven was much smaller than she was used to, but these witches and warlocks were strong. She could feel it. They were pure-bloods, like her. Damon was bastard-born, and with him as powerful as he was, it said a lot about the power within this coven.

Dot elbowed Alaina in the ribs. "They wouldn't stop talking about you all week. When you called, their eyes lit up. All except Emily, of course. But let's face it, she is a living corpse."

Alaina looked at the girl named Emily. She had snow-white hair and pale blue eyes. She seemed miserable. A living corpse was an apt description.

"Do you think we can locate Morgan?" Alaina asked, looking at the clock on the wall. It was Friday night, which meant Noah was going to be home in an hour. The witches had to be gone by then.

"I don't know," Dot answered truthfully. "A lot of spells have gone missing through the years. Few still know how to do them correctly. And if Morgan is as powerful as the legends claim she is, she won't be found unless she wants to be. I could be wrong, but I don't think that's the case."

"We have to try," Alaina said with a sigh. "If we can't find her, we can at least figure out exactly what happened to Brenna and Morgan."

"Gather up, guys," Dot said, and the coven obeyed without hesitation.

They were a ragtag group. Milo was an engineer with a love for sloths. Alex had the sort of face that seemed permanently smug. Tiana was a cheerleader. Gerald owned the town's only gallery. Graham was a man in his mid-forties with commitment issues. Lilith shared the same look as Emily but had a little more spunk. And then there was Dot, who was a mother to them all.

"Take each other's hands and form a circle around

Alaina and me." Dot turned to Alaina. "They can't locate your sisters, but they can enhance our magic."

"Because they aren't related by blood," Alaina finished Dot's thought, and the older woman nodded.

"That and they don't know anything but basic spells." Dot turned to address the coven again, which now surrounded the two in the middle. "Lend us your power. Every morsel of it. We need as much as we can get." Dot took Alaina's hands.

Alaina was nervous. She was annoyed that her new coven couldn't do a location spell if they weren't bound by blood, and she was anxious about performing the spell herself. With the power of the coven, she would be the most powerful she had ever been. And she knew what power did to people. She saw it eat Zachariah's sanity.

Alaina nodded at Dot despite the coil in her stomach.

The coven started chanting. It was barely a whisper, but the floor beneath Alaina's feet began to shake. She closed her eyes, squeezing Dot's hands as they recited their own spell. In her mind, she pictured Morgan's face. She saw her sister's delicate features and cobalt blue eyes. Alaina's lips moved on their own. She was vaguely aware of a door opening and closing but didn't address it. Power flooded through her, and she drank it up like a kitten with a saucer of milk. It was exhilarating. It was wonderful. It was the sort of high that she could get addicted to.

"What the hell?" Noah's voice boomed through the room, and her eyes shot open.

She wasn't sure what he saw in them, but his own eyes told her enough. He didn't know who she was. Confusion snaked its way onto his face, and he stared at her. He just stared. Alaina didn't say anything, and neither did the coven. Their chanting had stopped, and she was angry at

Noah for interrupting. She was furious that her power had been stripped away from her so suddenly.

They only broke eye contact when Noah turned around and stormed out the door, slamming it behind him.

Alaina should have gone after him. It was what Lindsey would have done. But Alaina was not Lindsey, and she was tired of pretending that she was. This was more important than whatever she was feeling for Noah. She was sure it was merely the remnants of the feelings Lindsey had for him.

So, instead of going after him, she instructed the coven to start over.

This time, she was ready for the surge of power, and she did not let it dominate her own power like it had before. She used it to enhance her own, not to add it to hers. There was a thin line. A thin line that Zachariah had crossed all those years ago. She wouldn't end up like the one thing she had to fight against.

Once again, she started her chant, a chorus of words that were long forgotten to this world. It confused Lindsey's mind, but Alaina's recognized it.

She didn't know how much time had passed before she got an answer.

The answer was not what she was hoping for.

There was no way of tracking Morgan. There was no way any form of magic could. Morgan was more powerful than Alaina could have imagined. They were hit with wall after wall of wards. The wards smelled like Morgan, held her fingerprint. Alaina could tell it apart from a million witches. It was elegant and controlled. It was like a waltz, like a ballet, a well-rehearsed performance that was performed without fault.

Alaina opened her eyes, finding the steely gray ones belonging to Dot. They had a fire within them, something she never saw in Damon's. The gray in Dot's eyes was warm and comforting, like a storm outside a toasty room.

With their eyes locked, they knew what they had to do. They saw the same answers, the same wards.

There was only one person who could find Morgan, only one person who possibly had the information that they needed. That person was Brenna, and she was buried six feet underground.

It was the answer that Alaina feared the most.

They had to raise Brenna to find Morgan. But if this coven could barely do a locator spell, how were they possibly going to raise the dead? How could a coven of misfits raise one of the most powerful witches of all time? A witch who'd no doubt warded her own death to prevent unwanted resurrections.

The magic that was needed was dark, the blackest black. But Alaina needed her sisters, and the world needed her. There was only one thing they could do.

Delve into the deepest, darkest pits of their magic and raise the dead.

Chapter Eight

THERE WAS A SILENCE IN THE LIVING ROOM.

After finding out that Morgan wouldn't be found, and that Brenna had to be raised, the entire coven was both shocked and horrified. Alaina didn't blame them, she too shared this reaction.

To bring Brenna back... It was something she'd never thought of. She hadn't allowed herself to mourn the death of her sister. She didn't believe it had really sunken in that Brenna was dead until now. But to raise her? How on earth was Alaina going to do that? It was forbidden magic, the magic that Zachariah had been kicked out of their coven for practicing. It was dark and evil and was known to drive people mad. It had driven Zachariah and Damon mad. It was bound to drive Alaina mad. But what other choice did she have? It was the only way she could defeat Zachariah. Besides, even if she did go crazy, it wouldn't matter because Zachariah's death came hers, too. She was going to die anyway.

Alaina knew she needed to find Brenna's soul to raise

her and not some undead puppet. To raise a person from the dead required meticulous work. The flesh had to be restored, the mind, the organs, the muscles. Everything needed to be perfect, and Alaina didn't know whether or not she had it in her to do it. Was raising Brenna really worth it? Was there no other way that she could defeat Zachariah on her own?

Alaina tried to locate Brenna's soul, but it was as if her sister had already relocated somewhere else.

"Brenna would not have relocated her own soul if she created this coven to aid you when you come back. She would have known that you were going to need her and Morgan's help. There must be another reason why we cannot find it," Dot said, breaking the silence.

Alaina shook her head. "Brenna was way too stubborn to let her soul move on, anyway."

"Do you think Zachariah might have something to do with it?" Dot's question chilled Alaina's bones. It was something that she refused to consider. If she believed it, that would be admitting there was a possibility of it being true.

"Maybe," she admitted.

"Whatever it is you want to do, we are behind you." It was Milo who spoke. Alaina smiled and nodded in thanks.

"What we are going to do is go after Zachariah's agents and find out what they know. We are going to track down Brenna's soul one way or another." Dot was determined, but Alaina shook her head.

She looked at the group in the living room. Some were standing, some seated, and some sitting on the armrests. "You most definitely will not," she said firmly.

Dot furrowed her brow. "But…"

"But nothing. Zachariah is more powerful than any of you can comprehend. He is a murderer, a traitor, and much smarter than all of us combined. It is too dangerous."

"Alaina," Dot started. "If we don't take action…"

"Then we might just survive long enough to come up with another plan. No one is going after Zachariah or any of his agents, am I making myself clear?"

"Alaina."

"Dot, unless you want your coven to die brutal deaths, you are not going after Zachariah. I have seen what he did with my own eyes. What do you think he will do with a coven of purebloods? He is already harvesting people to enhance his power, and no purebloods, I can tell you that much. Zachariah is a predator, and he won't rest until he has ripped us all apart. He will not stop unless we are in pieces at his feet." Alaina's nostrils were flaring.

She needed them out of her apartment so she could think. No, she needed them gone so she could go after Noah. She didn't know what she was going to tell him yet, but Alaina knew that she needed to be close to him.

A sickening feeling took over Alaina's body. Damon must have felt her magic by now. He must have felt the surge of energy, the ripple in the universe. If he knew who he was, then…

Alaina sprung to her feet, eyes darting around wildly.

"I need to find Noah. You can show yourselves out. I appreciate your help, and I will call on you all again." Alaina turned to Dot. "Please, no, not go after Zachariah. We will defeat him, but we need more power. Teach the coven. They do not know enough to have a major impact yet. They need to be strong enough to handle their own in battle. Because trust me, there will be one."

"As you wish." Dot nodded a little reluctantly. "Be safe."

"You too," Alaina said as she turned and bolted to the

door. She had to find Noah. She had to be sure that he was okay.

Alaina stopped at the door to the apartment building. She didn't know how she'd gotten to the bottom so fast. She felt as if she were floating. Where did he go? She didn't know. She didn't know where to start looking.

The bar, Lindsey's mind suggested. It was where Noah went when he was upset. He never drank excessively but enjoyed the ambiance. It relaxed him.

The bar, which was where she would start her search.

△▽△

IT DIDN'T TAKE LONG to find Noah. He sat at the bar, nursing a glass of scotch on the rocks. The place smelled like crap, but it was cozy. She could see why Noah enjoyed it here so much.

Alaina examined the room. Her heart sank to her boots. There he was. Damon. He looked exactly like he had that night he'd stabbed her. His eyes were cold, and his face was set into a hard scowl. He was talking to someone, pointing toward Noah.

Crap, crap, crap.

Alaina rushed toward Noah, startling him when she put a hand on his back.

"Noah, we need to get out of here," she said, her eyes darting around the room. She could see multiple men watching her. They knew. They knew who she was, and they knew that Noah was the only way of getting to her. She had to get him out of there.

"Get your hands off me." He scowled and turned toward her. His eyes were blazing, his voice a little too loud for her liking. "Who the hell are you? You are not the

Lindsey I fell in love with. I'm not even sure that you are Lindsey at all. I've tried, I've tried so hard. I went along with your crazy theories, went along with the insane shit you dreamed up, and now what? Now you're part of some cult? What the fuck is going on?"

Noah," Alaina said, her tone pleading.

The agents were getting closer now. If they didn't leave soon, she wouldn't be able to protect him. She wouldn't be able to tell him the truth that he deserved. She knew he deserved to know what was going on. And she was going to say to him, she only wished she didn't have to do it under these circumstances.

"I'll tell you everything, I swear. I will answer every question, I will tell you everything, please just come with me."

"Why?" Was he frightened of her? No, a man like Noah wasn't afraid of people. He was fearful of his own feelings of losing the one person he cared about.

"Because there are people in this bar that want me dead," she whispered through clenched teeth. Noah furrowed his brows.

"What?"

"They will kill you to get to me so, please; we need to get out of here. Once we're safe, I will explain," she promised.

Noah took another swig of his scotch, not biting.

Alaina sighed. "That man over there is the one who killed me 300 years ago. He failed, and he is determined not to fail again. I know it sounds crazy, and after I tell you everything at home and you still think I'm insane, I will drive myself to the loony bin. But please, just come with me before something bad happens. I wouldn't be able to live with myself if something happened to you because of me. For Lindsey," she finally added. Anger blazed in his eyes. "You owe it to Lindsey to learn what happened to her."

Chapter Nine

THE WOUND IN ALAINA'S ABDOMEN SCREAMED IN PAIN. IT felt as if that knife was twisting inside of her all over again. Magic. Uninvited, tainted magic, licked the back of her neck as they bolted from the bar. She could feel Damon's energy, she could smell the foul scent. It was like death and hell had joined forces. What was that? How did something like that even exist? It was worse than what she remembered Zachariah's magic felt like. It was so much worse.

They didn't chase Alaina and Noah; instead, they sent magic after them. Alaina looked behind her to see that the magic had turned into ghostlike hounds. They snarled and drooled, coming closer to them every second. Alaina sent her own magic back to them, creating a box to trap them in. They weren't going to be kept in that thing for long, but it would give them enough time to get to the apartment and ward as much as she could. No one else could see the hounds. They were magic, after all. She had no doubt that this made her seem even crazier than she already looked.

Alaina slammed the door behind them when they reached the apartment. Noah didn't have the decency to look winded while Alaina gasped for air. This body was not used to running. It wasn't nearly as fit as Alaina's had been. She led a confused Noah to the bedroom where she locked the door behind them. Wards, she needed wards. She needed all of them, big and small.

Alaina's fingertips tingled when the magic left her body, her body swaying as she recited every ward she knew. She put up walls around the building, around their apartment, around the room they were in. She made mental notes of where the weak spots were and fortified them with even more spells. She didn't stop until she had nothing left to give. There was not a drop of magic left inside of her when she dropped onto the bed, exhausted.

Nothing was getting through those wards. Not Zachariah and definitely not Chase. It was as if they were inside a six-foot-thick block of concrete. They couldn't get out, and no one could get in. Not for a couple of hours, at least.

"Who are you?" Noah's voice sliced through the deafening silence. Only then did she realize that he was still standing, staring at her as if she were some sort of anomaly.

She supposed she was. Alaina was a witch, a demon in some cultures. Possessing more power than any human being should have the right to. She was more than human, more than ordinary. It was time to tell Noah precisely what was going on and what she was. She owed it to him, and she owed it to Lindsey. Lindsey deserved to be remembered the way she was before Alaina took over her body. She deserved to be remembered without all of the crazy.

Alaina took a deep breath. "My name is Alaina, and I'm a witch."

Noah huffed a laugh. "You believe that you're the woman from that dream of yours?"

"No, because I really am. The people you saw here earlier are my coven, and that pressing feeling on your chest, the sweet scent in the air is my magic. The people after me are warlocks and witches, too."

"Why do I believe this? Why the hell is this making sense?"

Alaina shrugged. "I think you knew from the day I woke up that I was not your Lindsey, no matter how much you tried telling yourself that. You knew I wasn't your girl-friend, but you wanted to believe that she was still alive, still happy, still Lindsey."

Noah sat down next to her, exhaling deeply. She turned to look at him.

"If I tell you my story, will you promise to try and understand why I did what I did? Will you promise not to lash out and send me to an insane asylum? You've seen the magic, you just witnessed it first-hand. You may not have seen it physically, but you saw it with your mind's eye."

He swallowed but nodded. That was as much of a promise she was going to get, and it was more than she deserved.

"A long time ago, I was in love with a man named Damon. He wooed me, told me things every woman wants to hear. My sisters warned me against him, but I wouldn't listen. Damon was my ticket out of the farm life. He was wealthy, he was handsome, and I was naïve. He convinced me to leave my coven and join his. Zachariah was the leader, and I believed every pretty thing they told me. They knew how close I was to my sisters, and they turned us against each other. The power of three bound by blood was far greater than any coven with 100 members. If we worked together, we could put an end to every evil plan, every plot, and despicable deed they did. They were smart.

They took us out of the picture, and that left them nothing to worry about.

"But my sisters knew. They tried to tell me, but I wouldn't listen. I somehow managed to convince them to join our coven. Now that I think back, I know that they only joined to keep an eye on me. They didn't believe in the cause, they merely wanted to protect me from it. But they got fed up eventually and left. I was heartbroken, but I had Damon, and that was all that mattered to me. I didn't need anyone else.

"One day, I overheard Zachariah talking. He was plotting something." Alaina shivered. "Something terrible. He wanted to enslave humankind and rule over them with an iron fist. I told Damon, and he seemed horrified. He told me we were going to run away together. That we were going to escape this terrible man's wrath. I went home and packed. I told my sisters where we were meeting and what I was doing. They deserved to know. They didn't try to stop me; I was old enough to make my own decisions. And they knew that I wasn't going to give in, anyway. So, I left.

"I met Damon at an old church. It was abandoned and had seen better days. Only, when I got there, the whole coven was there, including Zachariah. I turned to run, but Damon was behind me. I ran into his blade." A tear escaped Alaina's eye, and she blinked it away. It was the first time she had relived that night.

She'd told him the bare minimum when she had explained it as a dream, but this was something else altogether. The world was still so raw. Alaina tucked a curl behind her ear.

"They tried to harvest my power that night. The coven was chanting some evil spell, and there was nothing I could do to stop them. Upon my death, my power would be Zachariah's, and the power of three would have been broken. Without me, my sisters were two individuals. No longer bound, they wouldn't have been threats.

"I couldn't let them get away with it. I wanted to punish them both for the betrayal. I was more hurt by Damon's betrayal than Zachariah's, even though... even though." She swallowed her tears. "Anyway, I used one of my most powerful spells to bind Zachariah to myself. It was easy, with the amount of blood that seeped from the wound. I could have bound Chase to me, but that would have been getting rid of the lesser evil. Zachariah was the one who needed to be stopped at all costs.

"When I died, I took him with me. We weren't supposed to be resurrected. We were supposed to stay dead, as the dead are meant to be. But even in death, we were bound. I can only assume that Damon, after all these years, managed to resurrect Zachariah. The magic sent me to the closest, vacant body with similar wounds that would bind us together. The first time I woke up after my death was that day in the hospital."

"This is crazy," Noah breathed, staring at the floor in front of him. "This can't possibly be real."

Alaina chuckled. "Of course, you still don't believe me. If I show you some magic, will you believe me, then?"

"If you're going to pull a bunny out of a hat, I have seen that trick before."

"What?" Alaina asked, but Lindsey's memories took her back to the time they'd gone to watch a magic show in Vegas. Alaina rolled her eyes. "No, this is different. Watch."

With the single droplet of magic that respawned inside of her, she twisted her fingers and set the candle on fire. It wasn't enough, though. She needed him to believe her fully. Gently, she pulled the candle closer by invisible strings. It floated closer, closer, closer. He didn't say anything as she made the flame dance. Two figures, one male and one female. They waltzed without music, and she had to admit that it was one of her best performances yet.

"So, all this juju. It's real?"

The flame died, and Alaina turned to Noah. The candle fell to the carpet with a loud thump. "Everything I have told you was the truth."

"Is Lindsey still…" Noah started, rubbing the back of his neck. "Is she still in there?"

"No," Alaina said truthfully. "Her memories are still intact, but her mind is broken beyond repair. Her spirit was gone by the time I claimed this body."

"Why did you pretend to be her?"

"Would you have believed me if I told you otherwise? Would you have helped me if I told you that I was a witch? The answer is no," she said without waiting for him to reply. "There is an evil in this world. I had to get to the bottom of it, no matter what. I tried to keep you as safe as possible. I tried to keep my distance, to not make this any harder on either of us."

"I guess I had already accepted her death when she was in that coma."

"You knew that I wasn't Lindsey all along. You just wanted to believe otherwise."

"I suppose," he admitted, and they both went quiet.

Alaina lost track of the time they spent sitting there, next to each other, not saying a word. It was only when she spoke that the silence was broken.

"Noah?"

"Hmm?"

Alaina didn't look at him, her eyes fixed on the floor. "I still need your help."

"And you still have it."

Chapter Ten

ALAINA AND NOAH HAD COME TO AN AGREEMENT, THOUGH Alaina wasn't entirely on board. Noah still insisted on her sleeping in the bed, and while it was very chivalrous of him, she didn't like the idea. This was his home. His and Lindsey's home. She was a visitor, an uninvited guest.

Alaina had the gnawing feeling in the back of her mind that Noah was only letting her stay because she had Lindsey's face. It was a feeling she wanted to shake but just couldn't. She knew that he felt a sort of loyalty to this body, and she was exploiting it. She didn't want to be someone who took advantage of other people, but Noah insisted, and Alaina complied. She didn't know whether it was because she needed help or needed his company. Sure, Dot was willing to help her as much as she possibly could, but it wasn't the same. Noah was the first and only person she'd trusted since she had woken up in this strange world. He was the one who'd showed her the ropes. She felt closer to him; somehow, even though he'd thought she was another person the entire time.

Noah was different with her now. She'd catch him

looking at her at the strangest of times, and although she knew he was looking at Lindsey's face, she couldn't help but be grateful that he finally saw her in there, too. She was no longer a ghost controlling another body. She was no longer invisible, trying to blend in. No, she was herself again, and even though she had a different face, it was good to be Alaina again.

Noah didn't walk on eggshells around her anymore. He had become a confident man again. He didn't apologize whenever he saw her, didn't try so hard to win her back. He treated her like a friend, and now that they knew such personal details about each other, they were closer than friends. Alaina felt closer to him than she'd ever felt to her own two sisters. The sisters who always managed to snake their way into her thoughts when she least wanted them to. They reminded her constantly of her mission and quickly pulled her down from her cloud and back to reality. They really were a pair bitches, those sisters of hers.

She remembered why she'd wanted to get away from them in the first place.

The wards did their job, but it was becoming a tedious task to go over the wards every hour to make sure there were no cracks. They needed personal wards, wards that would protect them wherever they went. They'd been cooped up in the apartment all weekend, but Noah had to go to work again. And Alaina… She had to get back to researching ways to resurrect her dead sister to find her missing one. It was one giant shitshow, and Alaina didn't have the strength to worry about the wards, as well.

Alaina and Noah stood before the tattoo parlor that bore the same symbol as the records. It was a magical tattoo parlor, Dot had informed them, and could do what no other parlor in the country could. In essence, the artists could ink wards into their skin to keep them protected as long as the skin was attached to their bodies. Alaina shuddered to think what Zachariah would do if he got his hands on them. Magic might not work on them, but blades would. And he would carve the symbols from their skin to get the message across. The crazy bastard.

Alaina could only hope it never got that far. She'd get her sisters back, and then there was no stopping them. Zachariah's reign of terror would end; they'd make sure of it.

"Are you sure this is a good idea?" Noah asked nervously, shifting from foot to foot. Alaina rolled her eyes.

"You are willing to help a 300-year-old witch defeat a 300-year-old warlock in a battle to the death, but a little ink scares you?"

Noah scowled at her. "I don't like needles."

"Don't be a wuss. Far worse things will happen to you if you don't suck it up and get these wards." There was humor in Alaina's voice, but her words were laced with a warning.

It was enough to settle Noah's nerves, at least from what Alaina could tell. He was good at putting on a mask to disguise his feelings, but Alaina was even better at recognizing those masks. She knew he was still anxious, but he was determined to see this through. This adventure had become a way for him to cope with the heartache. He'd lost Lindsey twice now, and this was the only thing keeping him sane. Alaina didn't care what his reasons were for helping her; all that mattered was that he did.

With determination, Noah stepped forward and opened the door for Alaina. She smiled at him, reassuringly and stepped inside the parlor. There was music playing, with some kind of screaming accompanying the instruments. It made Alaina cringe slightly, but Noah leaned down and whispered in her ear from behind.

"Seems to me like they are making soundtracks with the screams of their victims and playing it for their future ones."

"That's very dark, Noah," Alaina snorted. Their laughter was met with a crowd of judging stares. Alaina bit her lip.

"Can I help you two? We don't do couples' tattoos, so if you're looking for that, I suggest you go to the tattoo place down the road."

The receptionist had neon green hair that stuck out in every direction, with green contact lenses to match. His lips were painted black, and the matching nail polish on his nails was starting to crack. Alaina stared at him from under her bangs.

She had decided not to cut them or pin them back. Instead, she used them to hide the scars on her forehead. She didn't know whether it was for her own sake of Noah's but had a feeling it was the latter. She didn't want to remind him continually of the accident. Wearing his beloved's face was bad enough.

"The name's Lindsey Abrahams," she said. "Dorothy said she spoke to one of your tattoo artists."

"You're Dotty's friends?" A voice came from the back of the room.

Alaina hadn't realized they were speaking so loudly. Perhaps this man just had a keen sense of hearing. Dot said that this was a place of the supernatural. It wouldn't have surprised Alaina if he used some sort of spell to heighten his senses. Alaina smiled at him.

He was bald, and his head shone where it wasn't covered in tattoos. They snaked down his arms, his neck, and his fingers. Alaina found it hard to imagine that this man wasn't covered in tattoos under his clothing, too.

"Yes, yes, we are," she said. "You are Philip?"

"The one and only." His grin was warm and brotherly. Alaina got a knot in her stomach. It reminded her of her brother from hundreds of years ago. "Come on through to the back. There's an open room we can use."

Noah walked behind Alaina as they strode through the parlor, getting strange looks from the customers that were getting their ink. Alaina didn't know if this was a parlor for the supernatural only, so she didn't say anything until they were safe behind a closed door.

"Alaina," the man started, and Alaina stilled, rooted on the spot. "I have heard so much about you. I can't believe you're really here. After all this time. Take a seat." He motioned to the two leather chairs in the middle of the room.

"Dot told you?" Alaina asked suspiciously. She didn't like him knowing this much already. Noah took a nervous seat on the furthest chair. Alaina did the same in hers.

"No, I can smell it on you. The same way I can smell the sadness on the bloke." Alaina could hear the smallest hint of an accent, but she couldn't place it. Noah glared at him.

"What?" Noah's face contorted with an emotion that Alaina hadn't yet experienced from him, and she couldn't place a finger on what it was.

The man pointed to his ears, which were slightly pointed. "Half pixie. We have heightened senses. Anyway..."

There was a knock on the door. "Come on in. Alaina, meet Josie, Josie, meet Alaina and, um..."

"Noah," Alaina helped him. The woman was petite, too short, and too small. Alaina could smell the magic on her.

"Please, call me Noah," Noah said, and Alaina rolled her eyes.

"Dot said you two needed wards, yes? Well, let's get to it, then." Philip clapped his hands together, and then rubbed them as if he was excited for something as he moved over to Noah's side. He pulled a tray closer, and Alaina saw Noah stiffen. She had to talk to him to calm him down.

Josie moved over to Alaina's side, and she held out her hand. Alaina needed a good number of wards. Some to focus her magic, some to protect her from charms, and some to keep her grounded while the coven enhanced her magic. She told Josie as much, and the artist silently pulled her cart closer and began tracing symbols all over Alaina's arm and hand.

After instructing Philip on which wards to place on Noah, she turned her head toward the man who'd helped her through so much and grinned. "I never pegged you for the tattoo sort."

"That's because I'm not." Noah scowled at Phillip when he wiped the area on Noah's arm where the ink would go. Philip ignored him. "Tell me something, Alaina."

"Tell you what?"

"Anything," he said. "What was your childhood like?"

Alaina bit her lip in contemplation. "Lindsey used to make you watch Little House on the Prairie, right?" Noah cringed in response. "Now imagine that, but a hundred years earlier. We had balls and curly wigs that we all hated but somehow always managed to wear when we left the house. We had to wear corsets and dresses that were too hot and too long. I remember wishing I was a man most of my youth just so I didn't have to wear those god-awful dresses. But at home..." Alaina smiled. "We had a farm, and we all had a job to do. Brenna used to milk the cows; Morgan collected the eggs and fed the chickens. And my mother and I used to tend the crops. And by that, I mean use magic to make them grow faster while my father and brother harvested it all.

"It was simpler back then. There were no machines, no bug repellent. We had to make do with what we had, which wasn't a lot. But it was ours, you know? We didn't have to pretend like we did in town. We didn't have to pretend to be normal. We'd heard rumors about the burning of witches, but we were careful. We knew we'd never get caught. The ones who did get caught were either traitors or falsely accused. You think a coven of witches would let their kin get burned at the stake?"

"Are you saying that the witch trials were a hoax?"

"No, no. That was real. I'm only saying that there was never any reason for them to believe that we were witches. We contributed to the community too much for them to ever accuse us of such things. They wouldn't dare risk losing our crops. It was too valuable. It was too much of an effort for them to do it themselves. Besides, none of them could ever produce the grain and vegetables that we did. Perfect tomatoes, mite-less grain. Our coven was a secret, of course, but even if they found out, they wouldn't have done anything to us. We were too powerful and too useful to them." Alaina remembered the looks she sometimes got from the townsfolk, but she'd never minded it.

Noah grimaced as the needle pierced his skin. Alaina clenched her jaw when she felt the sharp stinging in her own arm, but she didn't say a single word.

"Your brother," Noah started, scowling at Philip when he struck a particularly sensitive spot on his arm. "You never talk about him. You're not interested in finding him?"

Alaina huffed a laugh. "I know where he is. I have no need to see him. Not yet, anyway."

"He's alive?" Noah sat up, which caused Philip's strong hands to push him back.

"He is, but he can't do what my sisters can. Witches are more powerful than warlocks. And with three witches... He just kind of distanced himself and became a menace of his own. The more I can delay our meeting, the better."

"My family is pretty messed up, too," was all he said. Alaina didn't push him. If he wanted to say more, he would have.

"I hear there is trouble in the witchy world," Philip said after a moment of silence. Alaina nodded. "The power nexus has been unstable for a while now." That didn't surprise her. The nexus had a way of knowing when it was in trouble. If Zachariah was around, the thing that supplied life and magic to every magical being was his number one target.

"Zachariah is on the rise. He needs to be stopped before the whole world pays the price," Alaina said, meeting Noah's eye for the briefest of moments. It was funny how such a light-hearted conversation could take such a dark turn so quickly.

"There's an underground network of protectors all over the world. The pixies run the whole thing. We're good at getting into places." Philip wiped away some blood before continuing with the ink. "I will contact some of my people. Everyone is on high alert with all those girls going missing. We knew something was up, but Zachariah of all things..."

Alaina huffed. A network of magical protectors, eh? Who would have guessed that the pixies, of all things, would run it? Alaina was used to them being cowardly and weak. Still, they must have grown tired of being oppressed by the other magical beings of the supernatural world. Three hundred years truly changed things.

"Zachariah has been a pain in my ass since I can remember," Alaina said. "It would have been weird if it wasn't Zachariah causing these disturbances." Just saying his name so many times gave Alaina a hernia. She hated his name, hated what he stood for.

She hated what he had become.

He had been a boy once, a boy she knew well. But power had driven him mad, and now he was a crazy warlock, determined to destroy the world. He didn't have an ounce of compassion for humankind. He had once, but not anymore. Not for a long time.

Alaina realized that he had gone mad long before he'd betrayed her. Long before he'd had Damon betray her. She'd merely been too blind to see it. She was too blind, too stupid, and too young. But now, she knew. It took her 300 years of limbo, but now she understood. She knew exactly what he was and what he had been for years before the betrayal. She regretted, not seeing it sooner. Things would have been so much different.

Josie snorted, and it was the first sound she'd made since she had entered the room.

"The town had people on all major roads keeping an eye out. Some are humans with a knowledge of the supernatural. They let the network know whenever weird things are going on. Lately, there's been a big spike in weather anomalies in surrounding areas."

"I saw," Alaina admitted. "They're too coordinated to be anything but magic. But they don't contain any trace of Zachariah."

It was only when Josie spoke that Alaina formed a realization. "Maybe Zachariah has someone else who can do his dirty work for him."

Someone like Damon...

Alaina's blood ran cold. Why hadn't she seen it earlier?

Damon had a different sort of magic to him since she'd woken up in the hospital. It was darker and more sinister. Perhaps the reason she didn't recognize it with the weather anomalies was that she hadn't been looking for his signature at all. She hadn't even considered the possibility of Damon being able to do all those things. Alaina swallowed.

"Regardless of who it is, people are on their toes. I'll let them know who you are, and they will give you a free pass." Philip seemed more serious than he had a moment ago. "You are free to move around as you please. You also have the help of the network. All you need to do is give us the word."

Chapter Eleven

THE GRAVEYARD HAD AN EERIE FEEL TO IT. IT WAS haunting, and Alaina had the uneasy feeling that she was being watched. It was an age-old superstition of hers, though. She'd always hated cemeteries, and her sisters used to tease her about it. Ever since her grandmother died, Alaina couldn't step into a graveyard without the feeling of her grandmother watching her. But being here now, with Lindsey's heavy heart about the death of her mother, she could now feel two sets of eyes watching her.

Alaina swallowed her uneasiness. There was nothing around them. They were ten sets of ears, of eyes. If there was anything out of the ordinary, one of them would have said as much.

"You're actually going to attempt to raise the dead?" Noah whispered from beside her.

They were waiting for Dot to finish her cleansing ritual. Alaina watched as she neatly placed crystals on the grave. Crystals to deflect negative energy, crystals to enhance their focus, crystals that she had only ever read about in books.

This had to work, it just had to.

"No," she hissed. His constant questions were driving her mad. She considered switching his soul with Brenna's, just to keep him quiet. "We are using Brenna's body to locate her soul. We can't raise her without her soul. Otherwise, she'd just be a mindless shell."

"Was that what Lindsey was like?" Alaina tried her best to ignore the tremor in his voice. "Was she a mindless shell?"

She wanted to tell him that she was still alive, that the machines weren't what were keeping her alive, and that she was fighting. But she couldn't lie to him any more than she already had. She already felt terrible for everything else she has done and said to him. He deserved nothing but the truth.

"Yes, she was long gone by the time my soul entered her body. I suspect the machines were the only things keeping her body alive. There was no fight in her, no soul. She died on the impact the night of the accident." Alaina could feel the regret his body emitted but stayed quiet. He'd asked, and she'd answered. Why was she feeling bad about this? Why did his sadness affect her so?

She sighed. "Rather that, than the coma, to be honest. It's hell in there, being trapped in your own head. With the injuries she sustained, she would have stayed in that coma until the machines were shut down. It was time for her soul to move on to another life."

"That doesn't make me feel better about it."

Alaina's nostrils flared. "How do you think I'm feeling, hmm?" Her voice was rising, though she was trying to keep it a whisper. "I accepted my death. My death by the man I loved. I accepted it, and I was fine with it because I knew I took the biggest evil on earth with me. But then I woke up in another life, in another era, in the life of another person. Did you know that Lindsey was older than me? I was barely through my 21st summer. I have too many memories in my head for me to filter through. Those four years that she lived longer than I, those happy memories that she had? How envious do you think I am? How am I supposed to feel about her living longer than me? Having a man that loved her above all else while I died by the hand of my lover? If there is a pity to be thrown, it will be mine. Yes, you lost someone you loved, but so did I. I am trying to raise that person from the grave just to help me end my life again."

"What?" Noah took a step back.

"Our lives are still linked, Noah. If I kill Zachariah, I die, too. That's why he hasn't killed me yet. That's why he sent men after you and not me. He could easily have killed me weeks ago, but he couldn't. Not without killing himself."

The news clearly took Noah by surprise. Alaina regretted lashing out at him, but her emotions bubbled inside of her like a volcano. Things were becoming too much for her, and she couldn't stand the pity parties anymore. Not when she had reason to throw one herself.

"If you are linked, then why…"

"Haven't I killed myself yet?" Alaina's words were poisoned. "Because this time, I need to make sure he stays dead. I have to kill his soul, not just his physical body."

"That wasn't what I was going to ask," Noah said softly.

"But you were thinking it." Alaina turned around, addressing the eavesdroppers. "It's what you all were thinking, wasn't it? Trust me; I've given all of this a lot of thought."

Noah opened his mouth to say something, but his eyes fell on something behind her. Before she knew it, she was behind him, protected from any assailant that might have been there.

"There there," the smooth voice purred. It was female. Alaina peered over Noah's shoulder to see. The woman was tall and a few pounds over curvy. If the mole on her cheek didn't scream "witch," her crow's nose certainly did. "Dorothy, dear, why don't you calm your pets down for a moment?"

"Agatha," Dot growled, her cleansing ritual now forgotten. "What in God's name are you and your miserable cronies doing here?"

"I heard there was a legend in our midst. I came to help."

Alaina stepped out from behind Noah's broad frame, tilting her head to the side. "I don't remember asking for help."

"That doesn't mean you don't need it, dear," Agatha said as she examined her nails. Her hair was carrot orange and curled to the root. "If Zachariah is going to be defeated, then you need all the help that you can get."

She was right. The clown was goddamn right.

Alaina nodded in agreement, much to Dot's distaste. She ignored the woman. They truly did need all the help they could get.

They stood in silence for a few minutes, Dot going back to her cleansing and Agatha's cronies appearing from the bushes. Alaina hated all of them. Her patience was resembling a thinning sheet, and the sheet was close to tearing.

Dot called her coven closer, and Alaina joined her in the middle, right over Brenna's grave. Alaina's stomach knotted at the thought of disrespecting the dead so, but the closer they were, the better. The grass tickled her bare feet. Curse this woman for being so damned ticklish. Her old body was used to bare feet in the grass. In fact, that was the way she preferred it. Bare feet, with nothing between her and the earth.

"Oh, no," Agatha crooned, and Alaina's nostrils flared. "The closest relative must be facing east. Everyone knows this."

Alaina turned to her, smiling with venom. "I am 300 years old," she said, excluding the part where she had been in limbo for the better part of it. "I shaped witchcraft in a way that you can only dream of."

"What's wrong is wrong," Agatha said, and Dot's eyes blazed with anger. Alaina sighed. It didn't matter which direction she was facing, but she adjusted herself anyway. She caught Noah's eye. He was grinning at her from below the tree he was leaning against. And fuck him, too, for making this worse.

When they were finally in the position that Agatha had suggested, her cronies joined hands with Brenna's coven and started their chant. They were too loud, too overpowering. Alaina could hardly concentrate, but she tried her best.

She called on her sister, then apologized for the noise and called on her again. She could feel her sister, could smell the apple scent that followed Brenna around. She could feel the gentle caress of her hand over her sister's shoulder. She was here... she was here and ready to tell Alaina where she'd hidden her soul. She was close, she was so close.

The cronies chanted louder; Agatha's Hocus Pocus shriek sliced through the air, and Alaina twitched.

"Focus," Dot encouraged, her voice soft and soothing.

But Alaina couldn't. Her abdomen contracted, and she screamed.

The cemetery grew quiet. Her sister, Brenna's soul, was lost to her forever. Her negative emotions were to blame for the loss of her sister's soul. The negative emotions caused by the very people who came to "help." Brenna wasn't comfortable giving up her location. Alaina turned on the ginger crone.

"You." Her voice didn't sound like her own. There was a roaring in her ears, a thundering in her chest. The crone took a step back. "Get your circus out of here, or Brenna help me, I will turn each and every one of you into toads."

"Alaina," Dot stepped forward gingerly.

"We were so close. We were so fucking close, and you just had to interfere, didn't you? You just ruined the only chance we had at defeating Zachariah!" Alaina approached Agatha, who was taking a few steps back. The wind howled behind Alaina, and she knew how intimidating it was. Most witches nowadays had to chant the spells to use them. But the old witches, the witches like Alaina, merely needed a thought.

"Brenna's coven was enough," she hissed. "My coven was enough. Get your obnoxious ass out of here! I don't need to chant a spell to wring your neck."

Chapter Twelve

THE APARTMENT FELT TOO SMALL WHEN THEY RETURNED home, so Noah took Alaina up to the roof of the building. It also had seen better days, but the view of the town was breathtaking. A cool breeze danced through Alaina's hair, and she could feel the little pieces of hope she had fly away with the wind.

She wanted to cry. She wanted to track down that damned coven mother and turn her into a mushroom. She wanted to do all of those things but found herself feeling exhausted. She was tired of fighting. Tired of having to deal with things that she shouldn't have to deal with at her age. She was still supposed to go to parties, to find love and a passion for a career. She had so much potential in this life, and she was going to give it up. She was going to give it up for this world, for that damned coven mother, for Noah, for Dot and the coven. She was willing to give all of that up. Hadn't she earned a little bit of respect?

She couldn't stand feeling like this. This hopeless, this powerless.

Noah was next to her, not saying a word. She was

vaguely aware of him shrugging off his coat and wrapping it around her shoulders, but she didn't say anything. All she did was stare at the town and wonder what was going to happen to if she didn't stop Zachariah. What was going to become of the twinkling lights? Of the children, the people? The pixies who ran the network? The other magical beings that made up this world? Would he kill them all? Alaina didn't have to ask the question to know the answer. He would kill every single one of them without a second thought. And Damon would be at his side, cheering him on like the lapdog he was.

"You're too quiet," Noah finally said, breaking the silence that hung so thickly between them.

Alaina sighed. "There was a time when Zachariah and I were close. We used to steal my mother's cherry pie and eat it in a tree just far enough away that my mother wouldn't catch us. He pretended to be my betrothed to get me out of difficult situations with strangers… He was the one who introduced me to Damon. My sisters didn't like him very much. They always said he was a rotten apple. They teased him, and I would defend him, thinking that they were just being jerks. They saw something in him that I never did. They saw the evil within that I never could. This could have ended a long time ago if only I had listened to them."

"Who was he to you, Alaina? A friend? An old lover?"

"My brother," she said. Her words hung in the air. Noah didn't say anything, so she took it as her cue to continue. "He was our older brother. He was a lady's man, always making trouble. My father forbade him from seeing the local girls because it gave us a bad name. Brenna and Morgan ignored him as far as they could, but Jen and I… We just got along. I supposed it was because neither one of us fit in, so we forced ourselves to fit in with each other. Jen was the oldest of our generation of witches, so he led our coven. But he became addicted to the power. He'd have us pump him with our magic until we had nothing left. It became a drug to him. So he got kicked out and started his own coven."

"And Damon convinced you to join it?" Noah handled this well. It made Alaina feel silly for making such a big deal out of it.

She shrugged. "Yes. I also wanted to have my brother back. He was my only friend, and without him, I just had Damon. I wanted a friend, and he was all I knew. I suppose he only ever took an interest in me to alienate me from my sisters. The power of three and all." Alaina chuckled.

"He was smart," Noah commented. "He was a manipulative jerk, but a smart one."

Alaina snorted. "Not smart enough. He wanted to kill me to break the trio of witches but didn't think about the consequences he would face from the elders. He didn't think I'd have it in me to bind us together. But our blood already bound us together. All I needed was a little chant." She laughed bitterly. "I couldn't defeat him then. What gives me the idea that I can do it now?"

Noah shrugged. "Perhaps because you are a 300-year-old badass who can control the damned wind? I had to pick leaves out of my hair the entire way home." Alaina giggled, and when he was satisfied, he continued. "You are the only person in existence who went up against this jackass and lived to tell the tale. He sends his minions after you for a reason. He doesn't want to deal with you, so they have to. He knows you're powerful enough to stop him, and it scares him."

A sudden realization hit Alaina, and she turned to Noah, his coat blowing in the wind. "Do you think he sent Agatha to mess with the ritual tonight? Do you think he knew what we were up to? That he wanted to put a stop to it?"

"I don't think the look in Agatha's eyes was anything but fear," Noah said. "She didn't look victorious when you didn't succeed. Maybe it was just a sign."

"A sign for what?"

"A sign that you can do this on your own, that you don't need a dead witch to help you. All I'm saying is that maybe, just maybe, you need to stop worrying about your sisters and start working on yourself. You are more powerful than you think." Noah took a deep breath. "Now that I know what to look for, I can feel it, you know? I can feel your power. I can feel it pulsing in the air. It smells like you."

"I'm going to get us all killed," Alaina said bitterly.

"At least you had the balls to try and save us first."

Chapter Thirteen

Alaina sat at Lindsey's favorite coffee shop. The dead woman's thoughts were no longer influencing her own, and it felt strange. Now that she didn't have to delve into them while pretending to be her, the memories faded.

On the one hand, Alaina felt bad for neglecting the girl. She deserved to be remembered. But didn't diving into her memories cross some form of boundary? They were personal and intimate, and Alaina wouldn't have wanted anyone to dive into hers like that. She decided it was time to let go of Lindsey and become Alaina once more. She was still herself, only in a different body. She couldn't understand why she was having so much trouble adjusting.

The talk on the roof the previous night was still fresh in her mind. Noah's words, despite everything, rang through her. She didn't need her sisters; she was a badass on her own. Be that as it may, she felt the need to bring at least Brenna back to stand by her side. Two ancients were better than one. Alaina didn't know how she was going to do it alone, and she couldn't put the coven in danger. She would never forgive herself if something happened to them while in battle. They were all still so young, filled with so much hope. How could she put them at risk like that?

She couldn't, she just couldn't.

Alaina had to go back to the cemetery to locate Brenna's soul. Once she had that, she could raise her sister and, if they were lucky, find Morgan, too. If not, at least she'd have someone who'd already experienced death and likely wouldn't mind going back to it if they failed.

Her mind made up, Alaina finished her coffee with a purpose. She needed this. They needed to do this.

"Alaina!" The familiar voice sounded out of breath, and Alaina whipped her head around to see who it was.

Philip, the tattoo artist, stood in the doorway of the coffee shop. People were staring at him, but he paid them no mind. There were much more pressing matters than what people said or thought about him. He strode toward her, joining her at the table she was about to leave.

"Philip, what is it? How did you find me?" Alaina looked around the room.

"Heightened senses, remember?" he said with a grin. "I could track you even if you were in another state."

"Creepy," she mumbled. "Now, what is it that's so pressing you couldn't tell me over the phone?"

"Zachariah's agents are rising. Things are getting bad, really, really bad. If you're going to do something, it had better be within the next few days. I don't think the world is going to survive another week."

"What do you mean? How is that possible? There was no news a few days ago," Alaina asked, her heart beating in her ears.

"Don't ask me. All I know is that shit is going down. I also know that there is a way you can slow him down, you know until we can figure out how to stop this son of a bitch. There's a place downtown where the energy nexus is. If you can contaminate it..."

"I can slow down Zachariah's plans," she finished his sentence for him. "But why has no one tried slowing down the flow of the nexus before?"

"Because there is only one way of slowing it down."

"Core magic," she hissed. Of course. Her magic, her core magic, could do it. It would have been a lot easier with her sisters, but she might just be able to do it before Zachariah could draw all of its power.

"Alaina, Philip," Noah said, walking over to them. Alaina looked at Philip.

"I wasn't going to track you both down. Besides, your magic reeks. There are a thousand men in the town that use the same cologne as him. So, I called him to meet us here instead," Philips said with a smile, very proud of himself.

Noah reached their table, and Philip got up. "Well, I just saved you the time of calling him. You are welcome. Now you two can plan in peace. See ya."

With that, Philip was out the door, and Alaina was staring at Noah, who, no doubt, was mirroring her confusion.

"That is a very, very strange man," Noah said as he sat down in the abandoned seat. Alaina nodded in agreement. "What is this all about?"

"Zachariah is moving," she said sighing. "Philip claims we don't have long until the shitstorm is upon us."

Noah swore. "Now what?"

"Now I have a decision to make. Do I try to resurrect Brenna again, or do I go to Zachariah and try to slow him down? You know, buy the witches some time to band together." Alaina sank her head into her hands.

Noah sighed. "I told you last night. You are a badass. You can take him on your own."

"I'm afraid of dying, Noah," she admitted for the first time since she was resurrected. She wanted to live, to explore this new century. She wanted to fall in love and have a family. She was too young to die. She wanted to live.

"Seems to me like we are all going to die, anyway. Why would you want to die hiding instead of fighting? You've done it before, you can do it again."

Noah's words hurt her. She realized that he didn't care if she died. She was squatting in the love of his life's body. After all, what was she expecting?

As if reading her mind, he grabbed her shaking hand and kissed it. His lips were soft against her skin. "I'm going with you; I hope you know that. Your coven will be with you. Even if we have to slow him down to find another way without killing you. I don't want you to die any more than you want to. But I know that you won't be able to forgive yourself if you didn't at least try.

"You will find a way to beat yourself up in another life; too, I just know it. You will live an eternity with your regret. I can't let you do that. I won't be able to live with myself if I do that." Alaina's vision blurred with tears. "There's nothing your sisters can do that you can't. You're scared to face him because you're afraid of dying. But they sucker-punched you last time. They tricked you. This time, you can go in stronger and wiser. You can prepare. We can prepare. This time, you're not alone. I have nothing left to lose, and neither do you. We will do this thing together. And if we die, we will die together."

Chapter Fourteen

ALAINA EXAMINED THE AMULET AROUND HER NECK. IT WAS intricate, with sigils and symbols lining every free space. Philip had proven his worth at supplying her with a collection of jewelry, encrusted with protective symbols and spells. She looked over at Noah, who was sporting the same jewelry. He'd only complained once about it being too feminine for his taste. Still, after Alaina explained to him what the enemy was capable of, he quickly shut up and asked Philip for another amulet, just in case.

After her talk with Noah, she realized that she didn't need to kill Zachariah just yet. All she needed to do was corrupt his energy source. It would buy them a few weeks at most. But it was a few weeks that they didn't have if she didn't try it. There were witches and warlocks coming from all over the world, but it was going to take time for them to get there for the battle. They needed time, and time was precisely what Alaina was going to give them.

At least, that was what she'd told the coven and the pixies. She knew that she was actually buying time for herself. Buying time to live the life she could've had. She was going to die, she knew that. It was a feeling she had in her gut. But she knew that in the few weeks she would buy them, she would at least taste a little bit of the 21st century before she had to die to save it.

Noah was on board with this plan, even if he was still convinced that they were going to discover a means to save her somehow. He'd promised to show her all he knew. She didn't want to experience it in Lindsey's memories. She needed to experience it for herself.

"You guys know what to do?" Alaina turned to her small coven, her heart yearning to hug each and every one of them. Her coven, the coven that stuck by her even after they failed all those times. The coven that wasn't afraid of traveling to assist Brenna's sister.

"Keep out of sight and keep you powered up." Dot nodded, giving Alaina a tight hug. They were in an alleyway that stank like fish, but it was a moment that Alaina would remember even in the next life. They were in the city, so close to Zachariah that she could feel his power pulsing in her bones. She didn't know what she was going to do if he showed up, but if history was anything to go on, he'd send Damon to do his dirty work. Damon, she could handle. Damon, she had a talk about having with.

"Keep your wits about you," Alaina added when Dot finally released her. "Zachariah's agents could attack at any point, so stay aware of your surroundings. If you have to keep some magic for yourself to keep a ward up, do it. Don't give me everything."

"Be careful," Dot said before leading the coven out the back end of the alleyway, leaving Alaina alone with Noah.

"Are you going to brief me, too?" Noah joked but groaned when he saw her nod.

"It's your job to keep me protected. The wards will keep them from doing magical damage to us, but they still have hands. The pixies will pick off most of them, but if they get to me…" Alaina's voice trailed off.

"They won't get to you. I will floor every bastard that tries." He smiled at her, and for the first time that day, Alaina smiled back at him.

Stepping out of the alleyway, Alaina was met with something that she'd never expected. Before her stood an army. She couldn't tell what they were or what magic they possessed, but she knew who they were without having to ask.

The network. They were the ones who warned her, who made sure she was safe whenever she moved through the city. The grin on his face told her that he hadn't expected this number of people, either. They were close to a hundred, not a lot compared to the number of men that Zachariah no doubt had, but enough. More than enough. More than she'd ever expected would show.

She was elated by the sight, but her hackles rose as soon as she saw the red-headed coven mother next to the network. "What is she doing here?" Alaina asked, not wanting to talk to the woman directly. Agatha stepped forward.

"I realize that I overstepped a boundary at the cemetery, but hear you me, it will not happen again. I am here to fight with you, as is my entire coven. You have our aid if you would give us the honor of extending it to you." The witch lacked the audacity she'd had when she'd found Alaina and her coven at Brenna's grave. She lacked the obnoxious laugh, the snarky comments. "I will keep myself and my coven in check."

Alaina nodded. "We need all the help that we can get. Head toward the roofs of the buildings. You'll find Dorothy and her coven there. Do as she says and we won't have any problems."

The witch nodded, and her coven followed her into the shadows of the alleyway behind Noah and Alaina. Things were looking up. They might just pull this thing off.

"The network will keep Zachariah's agents at bay as long as possible. They won't get away easily." Philip bid his farewell, and the network disappeared into tunnels, the sky, and shadows. It amazed Alaina that they could vanish in the blink of an eye.

"Why do I get a lecture, and he doesn't?" Noah huffed. Alaina chuckled.

"Don't be a butt. Let's go."

Chapter Fifteen

ALAINA LOCATED THE CENTER OF THE ENERGY NEXUS IN THE middle of the park. The streetlights were the only things illuminating the night sky, and Alaina found it strange that there was not a single soul in sight. Did the humans somehow sense a wrongness in the air? Did they know that something big was going to happen?

Alaina didn't think it was impossible. Noah did say that he could feel her magic now that he knew what to look for. It wouldn't have been possible unless all humans sensed this power source and stayed as far away as possible. Even if they didn't know what to look for, it was impossible to miss.

The stench in the air was ghastly, almost like death itself. It reminded her of Damon. He was here, he was close. He was lurking in the shadows; she could feel it. He was coming. He was coming for her. He was coming to finish what he had started. What if Zachariah had somehow figured out how to...

She had to focus. The energy source was a tricky thing. She had to contaminate it, to limit the power draw from it.

She had to be careful not to cut it off completely. Otherwise, every magical being would suffer.

The fountain in the middle of the park, the energy nexus, thrummed when she got closer. It was in a state of panic. It knew what was coming. One wasn't supposed to feel it this intensely. The energy was supposed to be controlled, constant, and soothing. This was bad, this was very bad.

"What is it?" Noah asked, reading the panic on her face.

"The energy nexus, it's..." Alaina began in a panic, looking around the park as if for anything that could help her. "It's panicking. It knows what Zachariah is up to, and it's trying to retaliate. I can't control it."

"Can't you sing it a lullaby or something?"

"This isn't a joke, Noah," Alaina hissed. Her power surged, and she fought to keep it under control. The nexus was emitting too much power. There was too much energy in the air. And with her this close to it... "My magic is out of control. I don't have enough control to put a tap on it. I can either shut it down completely or leave it alone."

"What happens if you shut it down completely?"

"We all die," a sultry voice said from the shadows. Every hair on Alaina's body stood upright. That voice. The voice that she dreamed of every night. The voice that haunted her when her eyes were closed. The voice that haunted her when she was idle for a mere second. Damon...

Alaina's head whipped around, glaring at the figure that moved closer to her. Closer and closer, he came. The full moon illuminated his strong features. Gods, she'd forgotten how handsome he was. He knocked the wind out of her every time she saw him. His tousled hair shone and the gray of his eyes. Those eyes that once made her love him now bore into her soul. She hated it. She hated his eyes. She hated his lips. She hated him. Alaina's nostrils flared.

Noah took a step forward, blocking her from Damon's view. Noah was a good head taller, but Damon was over 300 years old. He had experience; he had magic. The only thing Alaina could have hoped for was that he didn't have a physical experience. Against the wards, his magic was useless. He'd have to rely on his physical strength to over-power Noah. By the looks of things, Noah had the upper hand there. He was in great shape, but after the injuries from the accident, Alaina didn't know how well his body would keep up against a competent opponent.

"The fact that you need a human here to protect you says a lot about you, Alaina dear," he teased. "You don't have the power to even attempt altering the flow of the nexus. Just who the hell do you think you are? You think you're going to beat us with your little army of pixies and ragtag covens? Think again."

Noah stepped forward, his fists clenched. "Screw you, dude. You think you can just come here and insult her like that? You're the bad guy, you know that, right? You have no right."

Damon laughed, ignoring Noah. "Why do you think your brother made an effort with you? He knew that you were the weakest. You have always been the weakest. Your sisters, they would never have fallen for the trap that you did. They are far too strong for that. You were chosen because you were weak. You were the easiest to kill, so we seduced you with dreams and promises."

Alaina's heart sank to her stomach. He was telling the truth. Her sisters had always been more powerful than her. There was nothing she could do that they couldn't do better. She was weak compared to them. She was the weakest of the herd, so the lions had singled her out. She was stupid, she was so, so stupid for thinking that she could do this.

"You are a pathetic maggot under Zachariah's…"

Before he could finish his sentence, he was on the floor. The blow came so quickly that neither of them saw it coming. Noah stood over him, his right fist still clenched. Damon swore as he rubbed his jaw, glaring at Noah.

"You'd better shut your damn mouth before you say something that will really get me angry." Noah tilted his head back to Alaina. "He's talking shit, and you know it. I have come to know you, and what he just said is not you. You aren't that girl anymore. She died when this piece of shit killed her. You came here with a new sense of self, with confidence and power. You are not pathetic, and you have every ounce of strength your sisters have, if not more. You survived; you are here. You aren't dead or in hiding. You have balls that neither of them has, so pull your sorry ass out of that pity party and get moving."

Alaina's bottom lip quivered. Damon made to say something as he got up but was interrupted when Noah swung his fist again. Damon dodged it but was sucker-punched by Noah's left hand. Damon doubled over.

"You said you're not powerful enough to control the nexus, right? Bind it to your blood. You go on and on about the power of three, so do it. Use the blood that you and your sisters share. The power of three." Noah was tackled to the ground by Damon but yelled at Alaina to get moving. She knew no other witch or warlock would step close to the nexus in its current state. It would make them combust. Chase was the only one Noah had to worry about. He was the only threat.

Alaina jogged up to the fountain, Damon yelling behind her. His words hit a shield that Noah had erected for her. A shield of confidence, of protection. Whoever said that humans didn't have magic within them? She was pretty sure Noah had an abundance of it. The mind she shared with Lindsey told her that she, too, was filled with magic.

With that thought, Alaina bit her hand open and plunged it into the fountain. She was binding herself to the power node. She bit open her other hand, too, using the blood to trace the symbols on the ledge of the fountain.

"Look at you, I," Alaina heard Brenna's voice loud and clear. "You finally grew a pair."

"Shut up and help me," Alaina hissed, the power from the fountain overwhelming her, dominating every sense. She could hardly feel the stinging in her hands. But her sister was there. Her sister was behind her. Perhaps Alaina imagined it. Maybe the power nexus was driving her crazy.

"The energy is going to kill you," Brenna said. Alaina could feel her sister's phantom hand, circling her own in the fountain. "It's too much for one person to handle." Her hand tightened around Alaina's. "But with two, the load will be shared."

Alaina felt the power leaving her body. Tears of relief ran down her cheeks, and she let out a sob. She was doing it. She was actually doing it. The energy nexus was now a part of her as much as she was of it. Power coursed through her body, making her want to giggle and throw up all at once. She turned toward the fight behind her.

Damon held Noah by the neck, his hands tightening. Noah looked at Alaina as if seeing her for the first time. Alaina felt her braid dancing in the wind as she summoned it. There was a storm coming, and she was the heart of it.

"I will kill him," Damon warned, and Noah's face went red from lack of air. Alaina was not going to let him die.

Damon had another think coming if that was what he thought.

Alaina strode toward them, a deathly calm in her bones. It was a feeling she'd only ever read about. The feeling that she had mastered her magic and became one with it. She was the magic, and the magic was her. Alaina raised her hand toward Damon.

"Fuck you," she said, and she snapped her fingers.

Chapter Sixteen

DAMON VANISHED FROM EXISTENCE THE MOMENT SHE snapped her fingers. There was nothing left of him. No soul, no magic. Nothing but a memory that would soon fade. He was nothing; he didn't deserve a spot in her memories. He was a mistake, a waste of breath. He was exactly like her brother: a waste of time.

Noah ran toward her, enclosing her in his arms. Only then did she realize that there was purple lightning in the air, a crazy wind that made the roofs of the surrounding buildings shudder. She took a deep breath and circled her arms around Noah's waist.

The lightning faded, the clouds now nonexistent, leaving only a slight breeze that blew away the events of the night.

Alaina could feel her sister's energy. She could feel Brenna again. Where once was nothing but an empty space, now was energy. Alaina didn't know how it was possible, but she had awakened Brenna. Brenna was alive again. And she was out for blood. She was hungry for it, and Alaina could do nothing but smile, knowing that

Zachariah would have to face their wrath soon. Brenna's temper was something to behold.

But with the feeling of Brenna, came a different one. A darker one. Zachariah...

She could feel him; he was on the rise. He was angry, and she was going to pay for the plans that she had spoiled. She was going to pay for the inconvenience she had caused him. He was the sort of person who always got his way. No one ever dared to say no to him. No one except Brenna and Morgan, and now, Alaina.

Alaina comforted herself in the fact that she had taken care of Damon once and for all. He was no longer going to watch her, follow her, and haunt her. There was nothing left of him to torment her with. She had defeated one of her greatest demons. Now, it was time to prepare to face the biggest of them all.

"That was amazing," Noah breathed, squeezing Alaina tightly against his chest. "This was amazing."

Alaina grinned, knowing that he couldn't see her face. She never would have given him the satisfaction of knowing how much his admiration meant to her. She was too proud for that. Still, it felt good. It felt good to have someone who was proud of her for once. Instead of someone who always broke her down. She realized that her previous life had only ever consisted of mental abuse. They had broken her, little by little. But now she was stronger, as they no longer had that power over her.

Noah pulled back from the hug, holding her at arm's length. "I hope you know that I am sticking with you. You're not getting rid of me as easily as you got rid of that other piece of shit. I'll stick with you until the very end."

"You don't have to," Alaina started, but he interrupted her before she could continue.

"But I want to. Don't you see, Alaina? This is the

adventure I have a longing for my entire life. I told you this before, and I will tell you again. I have nothing left to lose by doing this. You've let me into this world that I can't ever ignore again." Noah shrugged. "I also kind of like doing this with you. I want to kick ass, I want to see how this story goes, and how it will end."

Alaina grinned at him. "Fine, as long as you promise me one thing."

Noah looked at her with skepticism. "And what is that one thing?"

"Promise me that you will pay better attention to the road in the future."

To Alaina's surprise, Noah laughed, nodding. "I do agree. My driving could use some work."

She grinned at him, and he smiled at her. At that moment, she couldn't have been happier.

Not until she heard a voice in the back of her mind. The voice that had made all of this possible. The voice that had helped her so much.

It was Brenna's, and it screamed in pain.

Alaina knew she couldn't wait for Brenna and Morgan to find her.

She'd have to set out to find them.

Other Books by Renee Joiner

Jaeger Chronicles

Glen Cove

The Witch

The Djinn

The Countess

Magic of the Night

Raven Magic

Single

Tempest

About the Author

Renee Joiner has been in love with the supernatural for longer than she can remember, so it is no surprise that she is an author of paranormal urban fantasy. Although she discovered her passion for writing when she was only twelve years old, she didn't make her writing debut until many years into the future. Adventurous and fun-loving, she enjoys traveling to new places, exploring new sights and meeting new people. Thus, she delights in creating fantastical worlds that are sure to give her readers an escape from the real world while simultaneously providing thrilling entertainment.

Besides her special knack for writing, you'll also find a passion for metaphysics spirituality which she has been nurturing for over four decades. Renee hails from New York and currently resides with her husband in their empty nest—unless you count their three adorable fur babies—in Florida. She enjoys adding to her sea of knowledge and thus spends her free time learning new things.

To find out more about Renee Joiner, feel free to visit her **official website**.

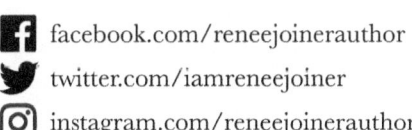

facebook.com/reneejoinerauthor

twitter.com/iamreneejoiner

instagram.com/reneejoinerauthor

Thank You..

Thank you for reading my book!

I really appreciate all of your feedback and I love to hear what you have to say. Please leave your review at your favorite retailer!